I0675290

DYING STAR

BOOK TWO: EXODUS

SAMSUN LOBE

Published in 2011 by New Generation Publishing

Copyright © Stuart Lee 2011

First Edition

The author asserts the moral right under the Copyright, Designs and Patents Act 1988 to be identified as the author of this work.

All rights reserved. No part of this publication may be reproduced, stored in a retrieval system, or transmitted in any form or by any means, without the prior consent of the author, nor be otherwise circulated in any form of binding or cover other than that in which it is published and without a similar condition being imposed on the subsequent purchaser.

www.newgenerationpublishing.info

For Kane

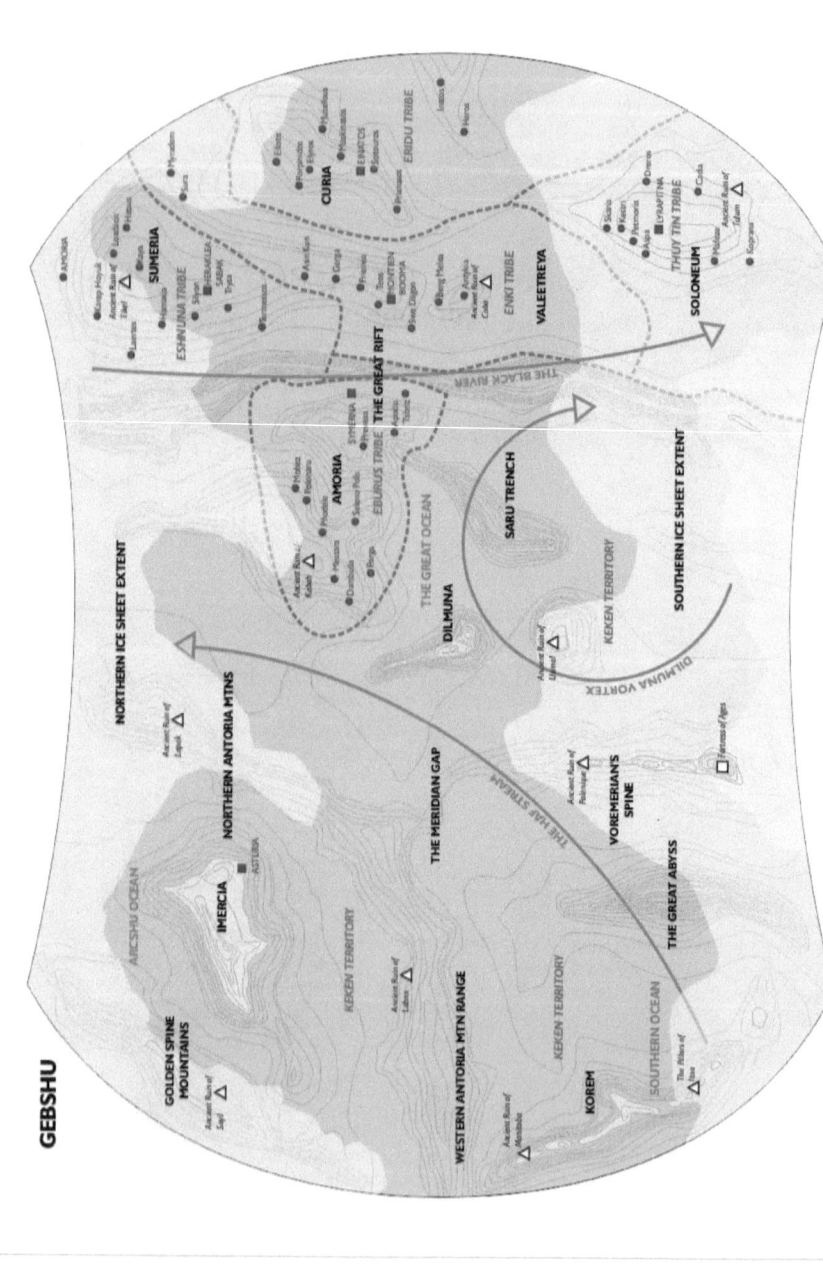

GEBSHU

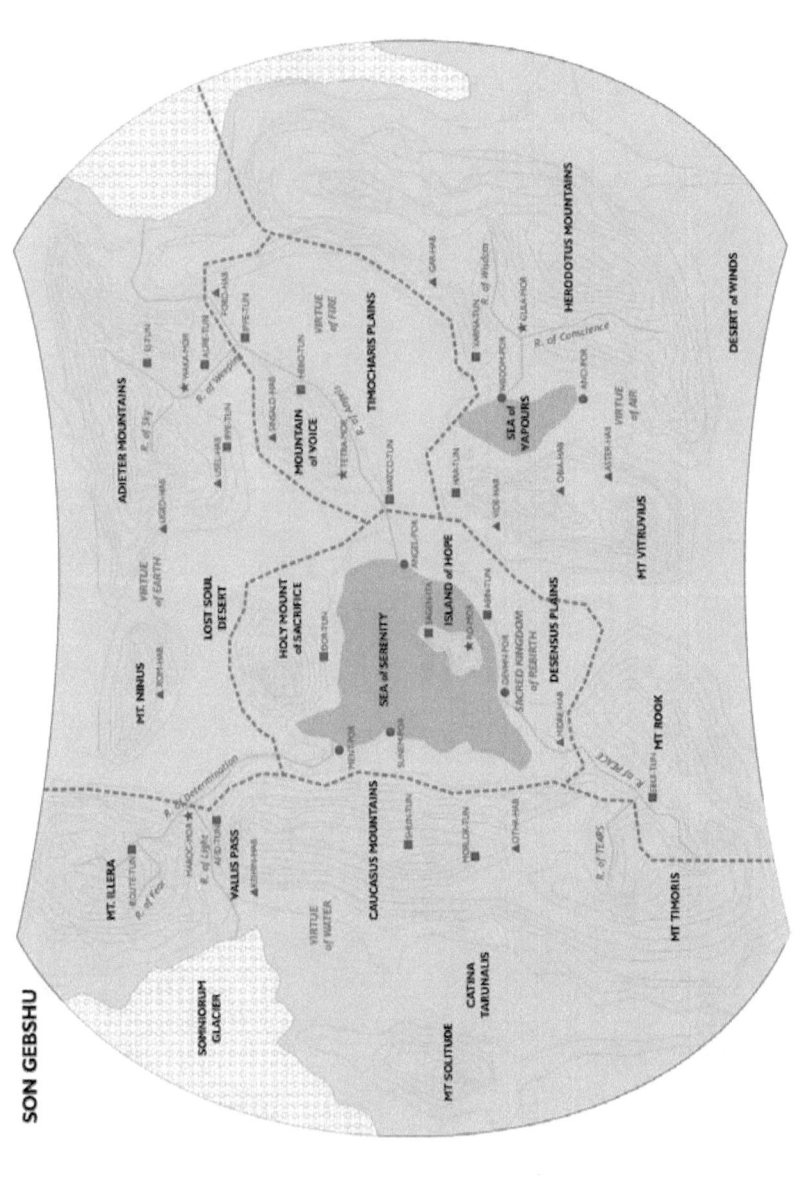

SON GEBSHU

DUMONII

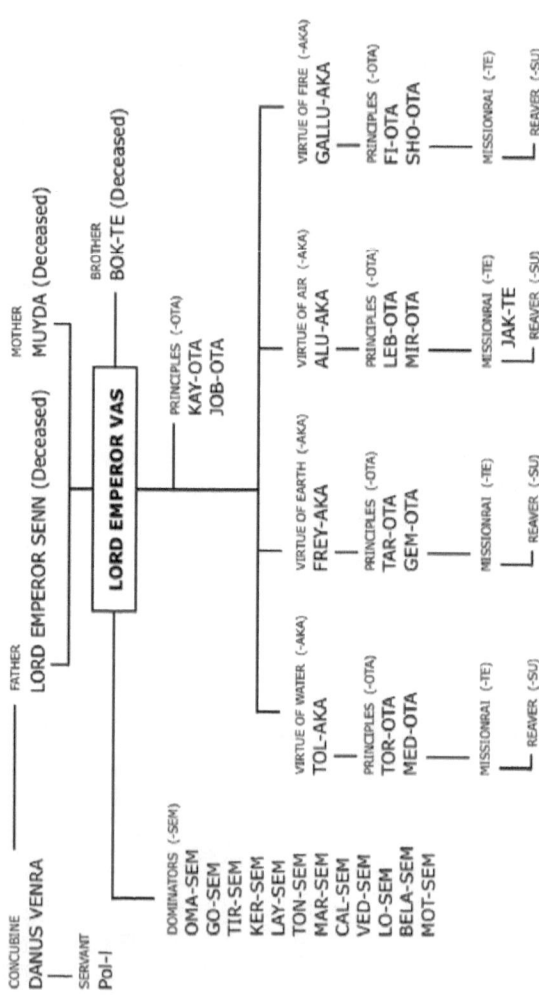

CONCUBINE
DANUS VENRA

FATHER
LORD EMPEROR SENN (Deceased)

MOTHER
MUYDA (Deceased)

BROTHER
BOK-TE (Deceased)

SERVANT
Pol-I

LORD EMPEROR VAS

DOMINATORS (-SEM)
OMA-SEM
GO-SEM
TIR-SEM
KER-SEM
LAY-SEM
TON-SEM
MAR-SEM
CAL-SEM
VED-SEM
LO-SEM
BELA-SEM
MOT-SEM

VIRTUE OF WATER (-AKA)
TOL-AKA

PRINCIPLES (-OTA)
TOR-OTA
MED-OTA

MISSIONRAI (-TE)

REAVER (-SU)

VIRTUE OF EARTH (-AKA)
FREY-AKA

PRINCIPLES (-OTA)
TAR-OTA
GEM-OTA

MISSIONRAI (-TE)

REAVER (-SU)

PRINCIPLES (-OTA)
KAY-OTA
JOB-OTA

VIRTUE OF AIR (-AKA)
ALU-AKA

PRINCIPLES (-OTA)
LEB-OTA
MIR-OTA

MISSIONRAI (-TE)
JAK-TE

REAVER (-SU)

VIRTUE OF FIRE (-AKA)
GALLU-AKA

PRINCIPLES (-OTA)
FI-OTA
SHO-OTA

MISSIONRAI (-TE)

REAVER (-SU)

Named Women have the prefix 'DANUS'
General population have the suffix '-I'
Special roles within the general population are:
REPLICATOR; MEDICATOR; SERVITOR

OCEAN TRIBES (Enki)

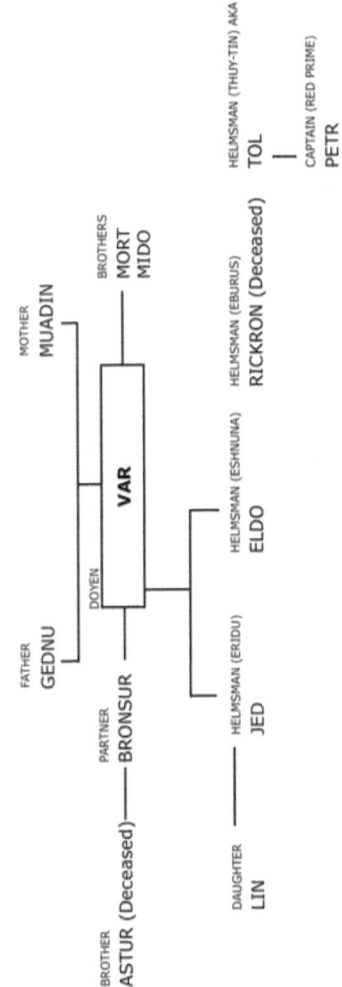

BROTHER
ASTUR (Deceased)

PARTNER
——BRONSUR

FATHER
GEDNU

DOYEN
VAR

MOTHER
MUADIN

BROTHERS
MORT
MIDO

DAUGHTER
LIN

HELMSMAN (ERIDU)
JED

HELMSMAN (ESHNUNA)
ELDO

HELMSMAN (EBURUS)
RICKRON (Deceased)

HELMSMAN (THUY-TIN) AKA Merthurian
TOL

CAPTAIN (RED PRIME)
PETR

FORMAL NAMES

Males have the suffix 'son' followed by father's name followed by tribe   eg Var-son-gednu-bay-enki
Females have the suffix 'aon' followed by father's name followed by tribe eg Bronsur-aon-vieto-bay-enki

THE MAGTA

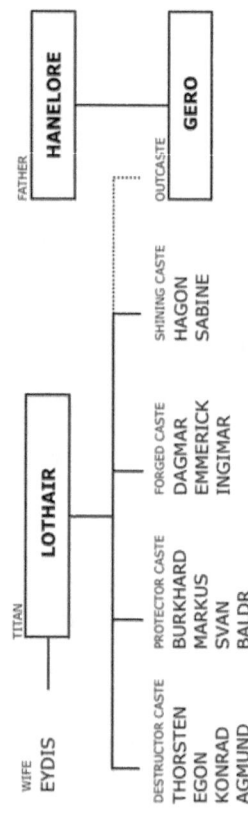

THE SHU SYSTEM

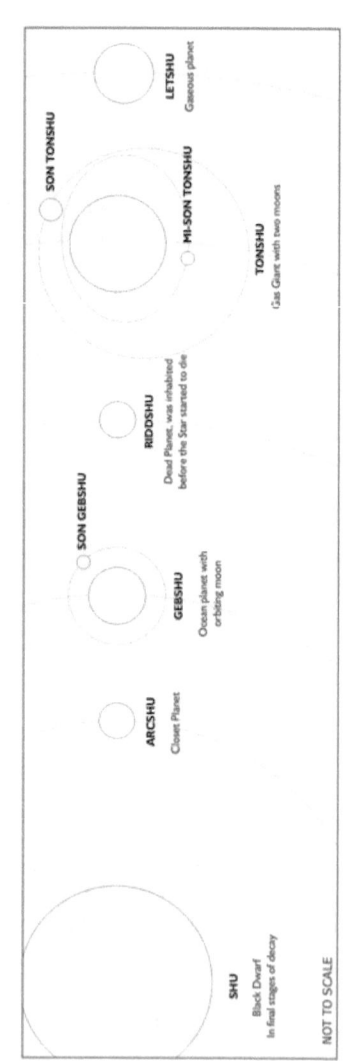

Book 2 - Exodus

Prologue

As the fingers of white light spread their aging grasp across the ocean planet, it seems as if the great star Shu would shine forever, but as it rises slowly into the sky it is a shadow of its former glory and its power so weak it cannot keep the darkness from enveloping its children.

Throughout its near immortal lifespan the fading star and its planets have been joined in the never ending embrace of change. This unbreakable bond continues as Shu enters the final stage of its life - death.

The massive ice sheets spread further into the oceans with every rotation. The creatures of the sea flee before it like some devastating harbinger. Those above the ocean fare no better as the temperatures plummet, harvests fail, and the air becomes choked with snow.

As the eternal cycle unfolds there are those who can adapt. Those that, despite the harsh environment, find a way not only to survive but to prosper. Long ago the tribes of the Deep South left their underwater tomb to forge a new life above on the pack ice. They alone now prosper as their icy domain stakes its claim on the rest of the world.

Those who struggle to embrace the coming storm still pray to the old Gods. Now, more than ever before, they turn to the deities who so often have forsaken them. They pray that they will awake and breathe new life into Shu and save them from the forever darkness.

In the black depths beneath the waves the icy tendrils reach out and wake another who has been sleeping for an eternity. The seabed rumbles on a tectonic scale as this bygone creature stirs the silt and slowly rises towards the light. The cold water stimulates its senses and revives its hunger. The leviathan crashes through the surface and bellows its defiance at the world. The Archaos is reborn and heralds the planets final step towards the end.

Chapter 1 - The New Emperor

The Lord Emperor Vas breathed deeply as the cold night air stung his throat. He stood on a small parapet looking out across the Sea of Serenity towards the mountains. The black kullstone of the citadel rose up around him to form the imposing fortress city of Sagen-Ita. It was a considerable drop to the rocky shore below and the small area in which he stood seemed to float unnervingly above it. He gazed, lost in thought as the small white caps of the waves lapped the coast. He remembered the last time he had looked down at this spot. The broken body of Tir-Ota had lain mangled across the rocks, his blood colouring the water. It all seemed like a lifetime ago when he had returned from the ocean planet and been declared Emperor. How could it have fallen apart so quickly? He breathed deeply again and cleared his mind of the melancholy thoughts. He could see the fires of the Virtue army burning all along the coast; he knew it wouldn't be long before the attack came.

He was jerked back to reality as the door to the private area was flung open. The Virtue of Water Tol-Aka smiled and walked across to join him. He placed his hands on the stone wall and looked over the edge.

"I'm not sure anyone would survive that drop" he said casually. The Emperor remained silent. After a comfortable silence the Virtue turned his head towards the Emperor. "I always knew that it would come to this".

"You didn't think to tell me this two revolutions ago?" questioned Lord Vas.

"Would you have done anything different?" questioned Tol-Aka. Lord Vas turned to stare out across the sea once more. "I thought not." continued Tol-Aka. "How long do you think we have?".

"This night, maybe the next" countered the Emperor.

"Your Principles and Dominators await your command my Lord." said Tol-Aka as he clasped the arm of the Emperor.

"I know, I will be there in a moment my friend." Satisfied with this answer the Virtue returned inside leaving the Emperor once again lost in his memories.

*

Two revolutions earlier Vas had emerged from the shimmer portal accompanied by the remnants of his father's forces and that of the late Virtue of Water. Runners were sent to all corners of the moon summoning all to the great temple of Ro-Mor.

The city of Sagen-Ita occupied one end of the Island of Hope and the temple the other. The massive shrine dwarfed the biggest buildings of the capital and stood as the symbol of power. It was here that all new Emperors were crowned. Two enormous statues of warriors supported the roof at the entrance and equally colossal pillars stood guard around the circumference of the temple. The sloping roof was decorated at regular intervals with carvings of gods, animals and heroes. Up close the light picked out the relief detail of the black structure and the workmanship that had gone into its creation was breathtaking. From a distance however, it was a thunderous black tomb, home of the God Emperor.

The coronation had been over in an unusually short time. The pomp and posturing of Emperor was a common and expected part of the ceremony. Vas had no time for the traditions, a point he made very clear to those trying to advise him otherwise. He had unveiled his vision for the future of Son-Gebshu, and there was clearly no place for anything that reminded him of his father whether good or bad.

One of Vas's first appointments was that of Tol-ith. He appointed the Servitor as the new Virtue of Water. He had quickly become a trusted friend and confidant since his father's betrayal. As the other stony faced Virtues took their seats around the ancient tree in the centre of the Sanctuary, Vas was confident that Tol was the only one here that he could count as a friend.

The five men all sat, each trying to instantly gauge the strengths and weaknesses of the others. The Emperor stood.

"Welcome my friends. I am glad you could make this meeting at such short notice. I realise things have moved quickly since my return and I know you must have questions. Let us speak plainly." Despite only a few rotations in his new guise, Vas was every bit the part. He was much taller than his peers and his muscular build set him apart from the principles and servitors. It was his manner that added the finesse. He was supremely confident, bordering on arrogant. He exuded this to all around him and it made those now seated in the Sanctuary extremely nervous.

The three older Virtues cast quick glances at each other, trying to silently re-confirm who should speak and when. Gallu-Aka the Virtue of Fire was the first to respond. He was older than all the other men. He had a leathery complexion from years of exposure to the elements. He had three strips of hair one on each side of his head and one on top, all tied back in a pony tail at the back of his head. The rest of his head was clean shaven. The hair he did have was dyed bright red. There was no mistaking the Virtue of Fire. His manner and temper also followed his title. Vas could clearly see emotions burning in the Virtue's eyes. "This will be interesting" he thought.

"My Lord" began Gallu-Aka. "My brothers and I are happy you have called this meeting. There is much to discuss and many questions to answer." There was a clear hint of aggression in his tone.

"Say what you must" countered the Emperor. Gallu-Aka looked across at the Virtue of Air who gave him a look of caution.

"We do not understand your decision to deny access to the resources of planet below us. How do you intend to feed the people without it?"

"The ocean planet has been a distraction" started the Emperor. "Over time we have become lazy and reliant on slaves to provide for us. As was proved recently this is a delicate situation. If we were to lose that resource then life for us would become very difficult. I am not saying we should not utilise the planet's resources, I am saying that it should only be as a secondary measure. Our first priority should be that of self sufficiency, here on our own world. Our fore fathers left that place behind for a reason. This is now our opportunity to re-kindle our once great civilisation."

"That was a stirring speech my Lord" countered Gallu-Aka sarcastically. "But exactly how do you intend to do it?" The Lord Emperor noted the Virtue's tone but chose temporarily to ignore it.

"The old food ziggurats will be repaired and we will build new ones all along the Sea of Serenity. They will provide ample food for the populous. " Gallu-Aka once again glanced at his companions looking for guidance.

"With respect My Lord, they have not been used for years; do we even know how to repair them or how they operated? Who will carry out the work? Who will man 'the ziggurats if you do get them working?" The Emperor un-phased by the questions replied calmly.

"We still have those who retain the knowledge of our predecessors. I have met replicators and medicators who have much to offer our civilisation if only we would listen. As for who will do the work.-we all will. The people of Son-Gebshu will find a new purpose in providing our food."

"And the people will just do as they are told I assume?" countered the Virtue of Fire.

"They will" replied the Emperor.

The newly appointed Virtue of Water, Tol-Aka, stood and nodded to the Emperor. Vas extended an open hand towards his friend.

"We have already scouted the old ziggurats. There are four that can be repaired easily and another six which will take some while longer. We have already identified those with the knowledge of how they operated. Within a quarter of a revolution we would have them fully working and producing food."

"Sounds like you have it all sorted" barked Gallu-Aka "My Lord, you asked us to speak plainly so I will. This upstart has poisoned your mind. He was but a Servitor. How can he sit here as an equal to me and my brother Virtues spouting this treachery?" The Virtues of Air and Earth both frowned as Gallu-Aka looked at them for reassurance. Vas remained calm.

"I am struggling to understand your issue my friend. Is it my appointment of Tol as a Virtue? Or my ascension as Emperor?" Gallu-Aka clenched his fists. The wiry figure of Alu-Aka the Virtue of Air stood and quickly moved towards his comrade before he boiled over. The Virtue of Air was taller than most men. He had a lean toned physique, long wispy white hair and an angular face. He had a pale complexion which was offset by his striking crimson eyes.

He placed his long fingered hand gently on Gallu-Aka's arm. The Virtue of Fire seemed to quell immediately as if his anger had been extinguished.

"What my brother is trying to say, my Lord, is that there has been much change in a very short time. It has been the privilege of the Virtues to counsel the Emperor on possible successions and matters of state. I assume that is why you have called us here this day?"

The Lord Emperor moved towards the two men. He seemed to ignore the Virtue of Air and his question and instead walked to face Gallu-Aka.

"Tell me Gallu, if you are brave enough that is, what you truly think? Do you think me worthy of my position as Emperor?" He leaned closer to the seething Virtue. "Well?" Gallu-Aka shot out his arm trying to grab Vas by the throat. The Emperor was ready for the move and blocked the grab with his left arm. The block turned the Virtue to one side and Vas Countered with a punch to the kidneys. The Virtue groaned at the blow. He quickly regained his wits and vaulted away trying to put distance between himself and his attacker. As he spun he looked up to gauge his position. Before he had lifted his head completely the Emperor's foot smashed into his chin, jerking his head back violently and flipping him onto his back. His vision started to cloud, but he could make out the Lord Emperor stalking towards him. He rolled onto all fours trying to regain his footing. The predictable kick caught him in the rib cage, cracking the bones. He winced at the pain but managed to stagger to his feet. He felt the iron taste of blood in his mouth and spat it onto the floor. Without a pause Vas hammered a roundhouse kick to the Virtue's left knee. The force of the blow dislocated the knee cap and Gallu-Aka buckled onto the stone slabs. The Emperor moved in close wrapping his arms around the helpless man's neck. He then jerked the Virtue's body upward with incredible force. The movement snapped the Virtue's neck. Vas released the lifeless corpse and the broken Virtue slumped over in an impossible pose.

The Emperor hadn't even broken a sweat. Calm but purposeful he strode back to the centre of the Sanctuary.

"That is the reason why I asked you here" he said quietly. The Virtue of Earth who until now had been a bystander looked unimpressed by the Emperor's actions.

"To kill us all?" asked Frey-Aka. The Emperor laughed.

"No, simply to understand where your loyalties lie. I will rule this moon, and I will do it how I see fit. This is not a democracy, my word is the law. I wanted to be sure that those who have my counsel stand alongside me and not against me. It is a simple question. You may of course challenge me, that is your right, as it was your fellow Virtue." He pointed towards the crumpled body of Gallu-Aka.

The Virtue of Air stood and looked back at Frey-Aka.

"I think I speak for both of us when I say.." He turned towards the Emperor his hair flicking in front of his face. "Go to the Depths."

Both Men stood and backed away from the Emperor. The Virtue of Water looked towards Vas for instruction.

"Let them go" he instructed.

"But my Lord..." complained Tol-Aka. The Emperor looked at the retreating Virtues.

"It is now up to you how this will end" said Vas.

"This will end with your blood on these stones" spat the Virtue of Earth.

"That is for time to tell." replied the Lord Emperor.

*

Tol-Aka watched the long line of soldiers wind their way into the distance. He had pleaded with the Emperor to allow him to join the expedition. Lord Vas had been quite clear that Tol was the only person he trusted to oversee the construction of the food ziggurats. Food production was the key to the Emperor's plans. Success on this front would comfort the population, reassuring any that were in doubt about his ability to rule and deliver on his promises. Plus they would need a huge amount of supplies to feed the troops now on the march.

The soldiers of the Emperor's Kingdom remained loyal to him as did the forces of the new Virtue of Water. It was this massive army that now headed towards the town of Angel-Por. The Emperor's strategy was simple, with the Virtue of Fire dead he would quickly march into their territory, rally the people to his cause before they had a chance to side with the renegade Virtues.

The main force consisted of foot soldiers accompanied by most of the remaining grounders that could be coaxed into life. The Emperor had quickly realised that the forgotten skills of the Replicators were going to be crucial to success. He had called them to a personal audience and given a rousing speech bestowing much overdue praise on the people behind the limited technology. The Replicators had lapped it up and sprung into action restoring the rusting grounder vehicles and some of the more mysterious relics. Some of these vehicles now rumbled alongside or were towed by the grounders. At the same time Lord Vas had sent the majority of his sea blades out from the island. They would approach the town from the sea and then support his force from the River of Angels as they moved inland.

Tol-Aka knew the importance of his remit, but he still wished he was at the Emperor's side. He stood and watched the departing army until the last units disappeared into the man made dust cloud. He placed a hand on the shoulder of Bar-I, the small Replicator that had been patiently waiting by the Virtue for instruction.

"Time for us to complete our mission" said Tol-Aka.

"Yes!" smiled the ever enthusiastic Replicator.

The two men headed a team of thirty plus workers who had all been hand chosen for their knowledge or experience of the ancient food factories. After only a short while they approached the first food ziggurat. The stepped pyramid was colossal. Built when the first Emperor had settled the moon, they had fallen out of use many revolutions ago. Now the once productive steps were so overgrown that the foliage hid the true outline of the structure.

The building consisted of stepped tiers rising way up into the sky. Each layer overhung the last doubling the footprint area for cultivation. At the front was a channel which ran the height of the pyramid. Its base was submerged into a deep trough which was fed directly from the fresh water of the Sea of Serenity. At the top were huge cogs that connected to a windmill. The wooden tower of the mill was still standing but the sails had long since fallen and rotted. In its prime the windmill slowly turned the long screw, which in turn raised water from the base to its summit. The water filled a huge stone tank and then through multiple outlets the water would cascade down over the cultivation terraces. The whole system was incredibly efficient, continually producing crops throughout an entire revolution. As soon as the crops ripened, they were harvested and then they were stored in the vast chambers inside the ziggurat. The chambers remained at a constant cool temperature preserving the food. The huge bio-system could easily keep a small town supplied. The regiment of pyramids that had once stood all along the shoreline and its river deltas had once supplied the entire moon. This was the re-kindled vision of the new Emperor.

Waiting at the base of the ziggurat were twenty or more soldiers and several hundred civilians. Tol-Aka wasted no time in organising the workforce. Each of the Replicators was assigned their own group and a specific task on the rebuild.

As the day progressed, the Virtue of Water couldn't help but be impressed by the drive of the workforce. Like an army of termites they crawled over every inch of the colossal structure cutting, clearing and mending, slowly but surely bringing the sleeping giant back to life. As the afternoon progressed, four newly assembled sails made their way up the steps of the pyramid. Under the watchful eye of Bar-I they were fixed atop the windmill. Bar-I raced around checking and double checking the interlocking cogs, satisfied that the work met his high standards he ran towards Tol-Aka.

"My Lord, I believe we are ready to test the first part of the system" he said trying to control his excitement.

"The first part?" queried the Virtue.

"I am still waiting on an essential part to complete the structure. It should be with us shortly, but for now I would like to test the mill."

"Of course Bar, please proceed." The replicator moved to a series of long levers. Each had a smaller lever at the handle. Bar-I squeezed the top mechanism with his hand and then pulled his weight backwards, shifting the larger lever into place. It grated and complained as the ancient metal gears shifted for the first time in an aeon. The strong winds filled the sails and they started to rotate. They moved at a graceful pace, but the gearing beneath span rapidly. The aching groan of metal on metal gave way to an oiled hum as the system found its old mesh. Bar-I grabbed the next lever and eagerly yanked it back. The huge metal cylinder then began to turn. The internal spiral slowly lifted the water from its base upward inside the tube. It was several moments before the assembled workforce could hear the water splashing inside as it rose ever closer. Tol-Aka climbed up a few steps and peered into the empty water tank. At first only a small trickle of water came from the outlet, but this was soon followed by a gush, and then with a constant rhythm the water flooded into the holding tank.

A cheer went up from the crowd, and Tol-Aka slapped the exuberant replicator on the back. Bar-I explained to the Virtue how the water would flow along the channels and into the cultivation terraces. As Tol-Aka peered under one of the tiers he noticed a rusty chain running around the core of the building.

"What's that?"

Bar-I smiled.

"This old thing has more surprises up its sleeve. I think that is what is left of an automated planting system. Each level has one, but they are all rusted beyond repair. It may have also harvested the crops." explained the Replicator.

Page | 16

"Ingenious" commented Tol-Aka.

"We also think the top stone that sits above the water tank held some sort of crane arm and inside there seems to have been a railed cart to transport the stores."

"This truly is an amazing piece of technology, to think we almost lost them forever." The Virtue grabbed the stone lip to pull himself up and as he did he spotted a flat crystal embedded into the stone. "And this... I suppose this has some function also?"

Bar-I beamed with satisfaction.

"It does. There are thousands of them all over the structure all linked by holes through the stones. This is its crowning glory. Bar-I looked down the steps of the pyramid and his excitement grew still further.

"What is it?" asked the Virtue.

"This is what we have been really waiting for" exclaimed Bar-I. Struggling up the steps was a large man carrying something very heavy wrapped in cloth. He was holding it and treating it like a delicate infant. As he approached the replicator he carefully peeled back a corner of the cloth. The light caught the hidden crystal and white light exploded from it. Bar-I covered his eyes.

"Cover it up!" he yelled. The Virtue watched puzzled as the two men climbed to the very summit of the ziggurat. They carefully lowered the giant crystal into a purpose made fissure in the stone all the while keeping the cloth covering the gem.

"Are you ready?" shouted Bar-I.

"What is it?" replied Tol-Aka. Without replying he whipped the cover away. The light from Shu poured into the faceted crystal. The tapered shape concentrating the light as it shot out down through the pyramid reflecting off the thousands of inset crystals and mirrors. The myriad of inter-connecting tubes allowed the light to illuminate each layer. The whole pyramid glowed with stunning white light like the gods themselves had given it life.

Tol-Aka just stared, dumbstruck.

"It's amazing" he said finally.

"My grandfather referred to them as the food beacons. I thought there must have been a good reason for it! Apparently the light and heat speeds up the whole growing process."

"It's amazing" said Tol-Aka.

As evening approached the army of workers toiled as the radiant pyramid slowly lost its lustrous glow. The Emperor's strategy for the future of Son Geb-Shu was unfolding as planned.

*

The long line of soldiers reached the estuary town of Angel-Por just before dusk. They had expected the renegade Virtues to put up some form of resistance, but as the scouts rolled through the outskirts, what awaited them was worse than anything they could have imagined.

The Emperor and the main force waited just outside the town. He stood on top of the grounder his hands shielding his eyes scouring the buildings for a sign of his scouts. The town of Angel-Por was a strategic location, positioned as it was on the River of Angel's estuary. It controlled access into the heart of the lands governed by the Virtues of Fire and Earth. Although part of the Emperor's own domain he had expected a battle to secure it. The eerie quiet worried him, but admitting to himself that the strategy of the traitorous Virtues eluded him, troubled him more.

He squinted into the distance, as he caught sight of movement. The scout vehicle, a smaller and quicker version of the grounder, sped between the buildings and out towards the waiting force. The Emperor vaulted from the vehicle and raced out to meet the returning soldiers. His heavily armoured retinue of Dominators followed closely at his side.

The Reaver Scout climbed out from the cab and slammed his forearm against his chest in salute to the Emperor. He was pale and shaking.

"What is it?" demanded Lord Vas.

"My Lord" The soldier gulped. "The town is entirely empty. There are no signs of the population and no signs of a struggle all except..." his voice trailed off.

"Except what?" enquired the Emperor.

"I think you should see for yourself." replied the Reaver.

"Tir-Sem, Oma-Sem with me, the rest of you will remain here. Follow in if we are not back before nightfall" ordered the Emperor.

The Emperor and his two Dominators jumped on the back of the scout vehicle and travelled back towards the ghost town. Vas scanned the streets and houses as they passed for any signs of life, but there was nothing. As they entered the central town square the Emperor could see the reason for the scout's demeanour. He called a halt, and climbed down off the vehicle. He walked out towards the centre of the square.

There were three tall wooden stakes. Bodies hung impaled on both the outer staves whilst the central pole held a severed head. At the base were what looked like the rest of the body torn into two separate pieces. The Lord Emperor moved towards the central stake. He looked down as the bloody sand stuck to his armoured feet. He then glanced up slowly at the decapitated head. The pale tortured grimace betrayed the victim's last moments.

"It is the local administrator" said the Emperor. "I met him once a few revolutions ago."

The Dominator Oma-Sem stood alongside the Emperor.

"What do you think they are trying to achieve by this my Lord? And where are all the people?"

"Perhaps this is a message, perhaps they are trying to instil fear, or perhaps they have lost their minds, whatever it is they will soon lose their heads. Get these men down and burn the remains. Tir, organise a thorough search of the town, I want those people found."

It was deep into the night before the search teams reported back to the Emperor. There were no further bodies alive or dead. Lord Vas had instructed his main force to move around the town and head up the river valley towards the city of Watco-Tun. He had no intention of slowing his advance and, as the events of Angel-Por had happened recently, he wanted to catch them unaware. For the second time in a rotation he would be one step behind.

The armoured convoy rumbled slowly into the outskirts of the City. It was difficult to make anything out in the gloom, but ahead in the street there was definitely something. The edge of the buildings appeared to undulate, gradually moving as if alive. A Dominator swiftly passed the viewers to the Emperor. He held them up to his eyes and carefully adjusted the range finder.

"I think we have found the missing population" sighed the Emperor.

"What is it?" asked Oma-Sem.

"They have chained the civilians from Angel-Por together; they are forming a human shield around the city. They look to be four to five deep on the main approaches."

"What are your orders my Lord?" questioned the Dominator, seemingly unaffected by the situation.

The Emperor knew that the fleeing Virtues would test his resolve at every turn. This was a simple test. Would he be ruthless enough to bombard the city, killing the innocent civilians before he sent his troops in or would he try and save their lives at the risk of further casualties to his own men? He shook his head and laughed to himself.

"You fool" muttered the Emperor.

"My Lord?" asked Oma-Sem.

"Deploy a small contingent here and at far side of the city. Ensure they are far enough away to avoid any sniper fire or skirmishes. They are not to engage the enemy unless they break from the city and try to escape."

"Yes, my Lord," replied the young Dominator, looking puzzled.

"This is simply a delaying tactic; the traitorous Virtues are close; the more time we spend here the more time they will have to prepare their defences. It could take several rotations to clear that rat hole, time we don't have. The main force will take a wide berth of the city. We will march on the temple at Tetra-Mor at first light. We can revisit this situation once we have completed our main objective. Once they have been cut off from their main force they will be an easy target."

The Dominator smiled with understanding. Perhaps this was the Emperor that would rekindle the fire of the Dumonii. The Dominator strode away with fierce pride burning in his chest as he barked orders to his men.

*

From one of the outlying buildings in the city Principal Tir-Ota edged his way towards the opening. He moved silently as he carefully peered out through the glassless window. He held a scope to his eye, the cold metal initially stinging his skin. Even in the gloom of the night he could see the dust cloud billowing out behind the moving column. He watched in total silence, unmoving from his position until he was confident of his intelligence.

Tir-Ota collapsed the scope and slid it into his pocket. He carefully crawled along the dusty floor and through the inner doorway. There were two soldiers crouching behind the door jambs. He nodded to them as he quickly scuttled away into the city.

The principal was a cautious man and even far from the sight of the Emperor's forces he kept his route to the shadows. He approached a large building near the centre of the borough. A quick dash across the street and he stood in the entranceway to the town's civic centre. The hallway was full of soldiers. They parted as the principal approached and one stepped forward to open the door to the inner chamber.

"Ah, Tir. We were beginning to wonder where you had got go" said an abnormally wide man sat at the end of a long stone table.

"I had to be sure my Lord" countered the Principal.

"Of course my friend, your unquestionable dedication for the facts is why I sent you. So what has the self appointed Emperor decided to do about this little dilemma?" asked the seated man.

"He is moving his forces around the city, I would surmise that he intends to by-pass us and press on towards the Temple of Tetra-Mor." The Principal held the man's gaze. "As you predicted" he added. The Virtue of Earth shifted his massive bulk back from the table and stood up.

"He may be a formidable warrior my friends but he is no commander." The Virtue laughed as he slapped his belly in a self congratulating manner. "Get word to the troops throughout the city, no movement and no noise. We will tear into their hind ranks like the tide upon the shore" he gloated.

"It will be a slaughter" said Tir-Ota.

"It will be annihilation" grinned Frey-Aka.

Chapter 2 - The Key

Var shuffled in his seat, he was squashed on either side by the two giants. He elbowed Gero.

"How much room do you need?"

"Don't blame me for the size of the seats. I had nothing to do with this build" complained Gero.

"Will you two stop moaning, this is a good match." The older giant pointed in the direction of the two combatants who were circling each other.

Var and Gero had wanted to go fishing. Surprisingly over the last few seasons the giant Gero had overcome his phobia of the water and now enjoyed being on it and in it. Their plans had been scuppered by the arrival of the last of the Eridu tribes from Curia. Since Var's victory against the Eburus and then the Emperor the ocean tribes had flocked to the small island of Imercia. The Eridu tribe had been arriving steadily over the past season but today the last of them arrived including the Helmsman and his daughter. Duty bound to entertain his new guests Var had suggested they watch the martial arts bouts in the newly constructed arena.

The arena had been Bronsur's idea, as were most of the new buildings in Asturia. She and Var had been pledged to each other shortly after the battle on Imercia. Ever since she had been the driving force behind the expansion of the fortress into the city it had now become. Var's attention span was limited when it came to politics and the administration problems of such an enterprise. He was happy to leave these decisions to Bronsur.

Every so often she would remind Var of his duty, and that as the Doyen of Imercia he was obliged to appear at certain occasions, chair matters of state and entertain dignitaries. Under duress he had agreed to meet and greet the new arrivals from Curia. He had suggested taking them to the new arena as this would involve the least amount of conversation and pleasantries.

The concept behind the arena had been a stage for public speaking and community gathering. Var had quickly seen the circular ring as the perfect venue to showcase the martial arts bouts. Since the battles three seasons ago Var had insisted that men and women were all trained in armed and unarmed combat. The old giant Hanelore had volunteered his services and had been training the population ever since in a strange form of unarmed combat he called Kayo. With many variations of kicks, blocks and punches it proved a formidable skill set.

Var enjoyed the lessons and had become quite adept although Hanelore had commented that he was still a little rough in his technique. Hanelore's top student Saul was now in the ring which was why the old giant was getting rather excited.

"Who's the other fighter?" asked Var.

"He is an orphan from the Eburus tribe; he is showing great promise; he will be an unexpected challenge for Saul." replied Hanelore.

"Eburus?" said Var

"He was only a child back then" countered Hanelore.

"Maybe" grunted Var. "I will be backing Saul though."

"Fancy a wager?" interrupted Gero.

"What? You are going to back the boy?"

"I think so" replied Gero.

"What is the wager?" asked Var

"Whoever wins gets to drive the blade when we go fishing later."

Var thought about it. He always drove. He loved driving the skimming boat. Still, Saul would beat this upstart.

"It's a bet" said Var confidently.

Saul moved around the ring with a confident swagger. He was Hanelore's top student for a good reason. He trained every day and thought about nothing else. It had completely taken over his life. Saul had an athletic build, was of average height but his most distinguishing feature was his lack of hair. Unlike the majority of tribes people who wore their hair long Saul had chosen to shave his off. Eldo, the younger fighter in contrast had his long locks tied neatly behind his head. He looked barely old enough to compete, and seemed somewhat frail compared to his adversary.

The two combatants bowed respectfully to each other and the match was on.

"That boy is in for a beating" said Var trying to goad the giant.

"We'll see" replied Gero.

Saul opened with a flurry of high kicks towards the younger man's head. Eldo stood his ground and expertly blocked or avoided the kicks. He countered with several quick jabs and then jumped spinning as he did flailing his right arm in arc trying to backfist Saul. The older fighter saw the move in time and blocked the strike with his forearm. As their arms met, Eldo dropped like a stone to the floor. As he did he swung his leg out in felling arc. Saul, caught by surprise tried to jump, but he couldn't avoid the blow and his supporting leg was knocked away toppling him into the dust.

Before Eldo had a chance to press his advantage Saul rolled quickly to one side and flipped back up onto his feet. He moved to circle the young fighter his pride wounded.

Gero looked down at Var and raised his eyebrows. Var just shook his head.

The bout continued with both fighters showing significant skills. Saul was solid and accurate, whilst Eldo was more fluid and relaxed. The two fighters clashed again in a close rally of blows each blocking and countering with amazing speed. One of Saul's counters passed Eldo's guard and caught him square in the chin. As he staggered back the more experienced fighter moved in quickly and grabbed Eldo's hair. He held it tight as he slammed his rotating elbow into the young man's nose.

Blood exploded from his broken nose. Saul released him and stepped away and then knelt down on crossed legs. Eldo sagged to his knees his hands clasped around his face. The master of ceremonies stepped in between the two men and held out a flag towards Saul indicating the win. A victory was decided by a submission, a knockout or blood drawn. Saul leapt up and went to see to the younger man with genuine concern.

"Hah" blurted Var. "I told you he was no match. Looks like I'll be driving again" he said smugly.

Throughout the whole event the newly arrived Helmsman and his daughter had sat just in front of Var and Gero and had been calmly watching and listening. The Helmsman turned over his shoulder.

"I have another wager for you" he offered.

"What would that be?" asked Var still elated.

"That my daughter Lin beats the winning fighter" he replied. Var smiled uncontrollably and looked at Gero who returned the smile.

"What are the odds?" asked Var.

"If she loses then we shall retire to our rooms and release you from any further duties to keep us entertained."

Gero nodded in Var's direction.

"That's a deal" said Var quickly.

"But.." said the Helmsman. "If she wins then we get to come with you on your fishing trip and she gets to drive."

"Still a deal" said Var without hesitating.

Throughout the verbal exchange the Helmsman's daughter Lin had looked straight ahead seeming unaware of the conversation on her behalf. She stood up, and removed the shawl from around her shoulders and handed it to her father. She turned to the two men behind her.

"I am sure your confidence is well placed." She then leapt to the edge of the arena and then somersaulted into the ring. Hanelore laughed, stood and clapped his hands.

"We have a new challenger. Saul, are you up for a second bout?" Hanelore announced. Saul looked across the ring at his new opponent and looked back at the old Giant and nodded. It was not unusual to see a woman in the ring, but not normally fighting one of the senior male students.

Var looked across the arena to the young woman who was now stretching in preparation. He had not taken any notice of her before. She stood as tall as her opponent, long silky black hair almost down to her waist. With her shawl removed the body hugging one piece skin that she wore showed an athletic body. She had tribal tattoos as did all of the ocean tribe, but instead of the solid, crude patterns that adorned most she had delicate swirls and patterns that wound their way around her legs and arms. Var found himself starring at her uncontrollably. Gero nudged him and whispered.

"Stop dribbling." Var snapped back to his surroundings.

"I .. I was just admiring the tattoos" he commented.

"Me too" said Gero with a wink.

The two fighters bowed to each other and then backed away ready. Saul rushed towards her and jumped leading with his knee. Lin stepped back gracefully avoiding the strike. She then flipped backwards bringing her feet upward into the exposed chin of Saul. She then cart wheeled sideways bringing her behind her antagonist. She thrust out a side kick turning her hips over as she did. The force of the kick hit Saul in the small of his back buckling him and then sending him sprawling into the dust. He stood quickly, but clearly hurt from the blow. He turned to face Lin in time to see her flipping across the ring towards him. In amazement he stood motionless as she flipped into the air above him and landed with her knees on his shoulders. Her momentum brought them crashing into the ground. Straddling the fallen fighter she let fly a lightening quick jab striking Saul in the nose. She then rolled backwards and flicked her hair in a wide circle as she stood. Anger was building inside the battered man and he clenched his fists as he stood ready to finish the fight.

The master of ceremonies stepped in and held out the winning flag towards Lin. Saul frowned in confusion, but as the mist of temper slowly subsided he could feel the warm trickle of blood running from his nose.

The Helmsman turned to Var and Gero, who were still in shock and awe by what they had just witnessed.

"We'll meet you at the harbour after lunch then" He invited.

*

Var stared out of the keep window. He and Bronsur had taken the top level of the old fortress keep and now used it as their living quarters. From the window Var could see out across the sprawling city and down the length of the island to the mountains at the far end. During his convalescence he had spent a long time in this room watching the civilisation he had sparked, gather momentum.

In the three seasons since he had first stepped foot on the island, the small Dumon outpost had changed beyond all recognition. The sea level had dropped by almost the height of two men which had exposed a vast area of land that had previously been submerged.

They had been overwhelmed by the influx of migrants in the first season. Thousands of tribes people desperate to breathe fresh air and witness the heroes and places of the many legends that had started the rounds. From the outset Bronsur had insisted that no more dwellings were to be built on the island outside the perimeter of the fortress. This ground had to be left for food production. The new settlers had not minded and had used the only build method they knew. The first pods had been built close to the shoreline and had been completely submerged by the sea. These and hundreds more were now exposed to the air as the water level waned. Hundreds more lurked just beneath the waves. As space became a premium the more creative builders had built on top of existing homes. The whole scene now resembled a colony of barnacles with the old wreck of the fortress at its centre.

The chaotic dwellings were linked by walkways, ladders and ropes and there was constant movement of people from one place to the next. From a distance the city looked like some giant sea creature that had crawled onto the land and was basking in the fading sun.

Var was incredibly proud of Bronsur. Var had lost heart after the battle with the Emperor; his wounds had taken their toll. She had nursed him constantly and kept his spirits high. At the same time establishing a form of governance and directing the many factions into a cohesive community. Var had certainly started it all but it was Bronsur who ran the show now. Var didn't mind taking a back seat; diplomatic machinations were definitely not his forte. He longed for adventure and his mind continually played out the trials of his past. He and the giant Gero now spent most of their time fishing, sparring and generally avoiding the work they were required to do.

Bronsur moved back the curtain quietly. She knew exactly where Var would be. She had lost count of the times she had watched him as he sat staring out of the window. She walked up behind him and placed her slender hand on his shoulder. She bent over and gently kissed him on the cheek. Var reached up and held her hand.

"Aren't you supposed to be meeting the Eridu Helmsman and his daughter at the harbour my love?" She had posed it as a question but Var understood what she really meant.

"I was just about to get ready" complained Var.

"Of course you were" she replied without any hint of sarcasm.

"I just have to put that thing on and I'll be ready." He inclined his head towards the bed and the contraption lying on it. Bronsur knew how much he wanted to complain, but he never did, not once had she heard him bemoan his condition. She knew also, how much he wanted to prove himself to be the man he had once been. One day my love, she thought, one day.

"Take good care of our guests" she continued "And try not to stare too much at his daughter Lin. I have heard she is quite beautiful."

"I haven't really noticed" blurted Var.

"I'll take that as a yes then. We have a banquet planned at dusk as a welcome. Just get them back to the city on time." She kissed him again and in a waft of perfume swirled and left the room.

Var smiled. His melancholy musings fading as reality stung once again. He looked down the scarred stump of his right leg. He scratched at it making the skin colour. Although they had won the battle against the Emperor, they had paid a heavy price. He had lost his best friend Astur and many others had died during the fighting. Gero had emerged from the battle covered in cuts, but the veteran warrior had healed within a short time. Var had not been so lucky. He had sustained a multitude of injuries in his encounter with the Emperor, the worst being the smashed bones of his knee and leg. Although Hanelore had done what he could with the knee it had become inflamed. His foot had turned crimson and the colour had started to climb his calf. With Var in a deep fever, Hanelore had amputated his leg just below the knee. The drastic operation had saved his life and he recovered from the wound quickly, at least physically.

He pushed himself up from the chair and hopped to the bed. He swung himself down and reached to grab his prosthetic limb. His new leg was truly a work of wonder. Hanelore had spent countless hours crafting it. The limb was a mixture of metal and wood, with a sprung foot and leather harness. The care that had gone into its manufacture was clear. Var knew Hanelore had put all his knowledge into its creation as some kind of recompense for the guilt he carried. Var bore him no ill will but was still ever thankful for the work of art that was his replacement leg.

He strapped on the device around his knee, and stood putting his weight forward. It had taken him some time to get used to wearing it, but now it had become an extension of his body and apart from a slight change in his gait it did not hamper him physically at all.

*

The rest of the fishing party were patiently waiting on the quayside as Var raced towards them. It was quite a journey to the harbour from the fortress. The harbour walls had been extended three times over the last few seasons as the retreating ocean left the boats beached. The latest additions splayed out following higher ground to either side of a deep channel. It would be some time before the current harbour became dry.

"Glad you could join us" smiled Gero. "Were you washing your hair or something?" joked the giant.

"It's not that time of the year already is it?" replied Var.

The elder Helmsman looked at the two men and then at his daughter.

"These are the heroes you were so keen to meet?" he asked.

"Hush father" snapped Lin blushing.

Gero jumped on the deck of the sea blade and his vast weight caused the craft to rock on the water. Gero stepped across onto the rail of the boat and offered his hand to Lin. She smiled and leapt passed Var and landed lightly on the deck. Var looked at the ageing Helmsman.

"Are you going to do that also?" he asked raising his eyebrows.

The old man grabbed Var's hand glaring at him constantly as he was helped aboard.

"What is this machine?" asked Lin.

"They were left here by the Dumon. There used be a lot more, a whole fleet in fact. We know how they operate but once something breaks we are a bit stuck. We have managed to keep this one going by removing parts from the few remaining others, but we don't really understand how they work. It won't be long before this one goes the same way as the others." Var pointed out at the rusting hulks of two other sea blades part submerged in the harbour.

"It is safe though?" questioned the Helmsman.

"Stop worrying father" interrupted Lin "We're in safe hands."

Var moved towards the cabin and cast Gero a sly glance.

"If only she knew" whispered Var with a smile.

The old sea blade coughed into life, black smoke pouring out from the exhausts. After several revs on the throttle the engine cleared its throat and the smoke dissolved into the air. The craft grumbled in anticipation.

"I believe the honour is yours" gestured Gero towards the controls. Lin stepped up to the wheelhouse and scanned the equipment. Var was just about to begin explaining how it worked, when Lin pushed the throttle forward and they lurched forward. Var grabbed the side of the cabin to stop himself from falling, Gero had done likewise. The old Helmsman was sat at the back of the craft smiling.

As the power fed the engines, the fans in the two stubby wings of the craft forced out air beneath them and raised the rusted metal boat above the water. The engines coughed once more in complaint before thrusting the sea blade forwards on its cushion of air.

"This is amazing!" exclaimed Lin as she turned the wheel wallowing the craft from left to right. Var stared open mouthed at Gero. Gero just shrugged his shoulders.

Much to Var's disappointment Lin's enthusiasm for driving the creaking craft did not seem to fade. He reluctantly showed her how to navigate and they set a course for the deep ocean. He joined Gero and the Eridu Helmsman at the back of the boat.

"I don't think she is going to let you have a go my friend" suggested Gero.

Var sat next to the giant and pulled his cloak around his shoulders.

"It's getting colder with every season" mumbled Var.

"Jed was just telling me they encountered the southern ice sheet when they journeyed to Imercia" said Gero cheerfully, trying to trigger a conversation. It didn't work. The three men sat in silence as the sea blade bounced from the wave tops.

The craft skimmed its way further and further out into the ocean, both Jed and Gero closed their eyes rocked to sleep by the constant buffeting. Var stood and approached Lin.

"I think we are nearly there" said Var making a conscious effort to stare at the navigation screen only.

"Great" replied Lin. "I'll go wake those two." Var took the controls and pulled back on the throttle. A garbled noise came from the engines as they lost power and began to idle.

The group struggled with the fishing lines as the vessel rocked violently on the waves. The skies had quickly clouded over and dark shapes now rolled across the vista casting their shadows across the ocean. In the distance the low rumble of thunder could be heard.

"We've not got long" warned Gero.

"We have to go back already? We haven't even cast a line" questioned Lin.

"The storms out here can get furious, even with the speed of the sea blade we should be careful. I have seen waves that would top the keep back at Asturia" explained Var.

"Ok then" started Lin. "We cast the lines, first fish wins and then we make for home?"

Gero and Var didn't even reply. They cast their lures from the back of the boat and held the baited lines in anticipation. Lin chuckled and joined them. Spots of rain started to fall and colour the wooden deck of the boat. Jed walked to the prow of the vessel to find cover in the cabin.

"What's the biggest fish you've caught?" asked Lin.

"On these lures - about this" said Var gesturing with his hands. Gero grabbed his arms and moved them closer together.

"More like that" he smiled. The trio laughed as the rain fell harder. Gero tugged at his line.

"Got something!" he yelled. He pulled back on the fishing lure, whatever he had hooked it was big as the line started to bite into his hands. He braced himself to take the weight and Var quickly jumped in to help the giant. In an instant the line snapped and the two men were sent sprawling across the slippery deck. As they recovered themselves a large black creature leapt from the sea landing in front of them. It was a kekken. The creature eyed the two prone warriors with teardrop orbs, saliva dripping between a myriad of needle teeth. The creature made repeated clicking sounds in its throat.

The kekken were legendary among the ocean tribes. They swam in large packs. They were intelligent fast and deadly. The depths of the oceans belonged to them. Var had met them before; it was how he had received the scar across his face. They had their own agenda and three seasons ago helped him to defeat the Eburus tribe. They were able to communicate telepathically through touch. It had been a long time since Var had come across them.

Lin looked terrified as the creature flexed its razor sharp talons and flicked its long tail.

"It's OK" shouted Var. "They're friendly."

Var stood and approached the creature. Something felt wrong. He moved his arms in the sign language of the tribes.

<<Friend>> he signed.

With lightning speed the creature slashed his talons out across Var's torso. Var attempted to jump back to avoid the blow. He moved quickly and avoided the full force but the tips of the creatures claws raked through his cloak and tore into his flesh. Var shouted in pain as he stumbled to the deck. The creature tried to press its attack but flailed wildly as Lin jumped onto its back slicing her dagger into the side of its head. She rolled free as the creature died.

"Friendly?" she asked.

Before Var had a chance to answer three more creatures leapt onto the deck. They snarled their hatred. Gero wasted no time: he grabbed a boat hook from hanging the cabin wall and launched it full tilt at the kekken. The power of throw sent the barbed metal spear through the body of the creature and it erupted in a spray of black blood from its back. The force carried the kekken back over the stern and into the sea.

"Get to the top level" bellowed Gero. Var was already climbing the ladder. His leg hampered him slightly as he could not feel the rungs but he made it swiftly to the top and turned to help his comrades. One of the creatures leapt forward towards Lin slashing its claws. She darted to one side and then leapt to grab Var's outstretched hand. With one movement he hauled her on top of the cabin roof.

"Gero!" shouted Var. "Up here!" The other creature was circling the giant, more cautious with its approach. The giant reached out one of his massive arms and clamped his hand around the creature's head, his fingers digging into its eyes. The kekken slashed at his arm gauging it deeply. Unflinching Gero dragged the creature into his body turning the threshing creature as he did. He wrapped his other arm around its neck and jerked them back violently. His raw power broke the creature's neck and nearly tore the head from its body. Gero grimaced as the other animal leapt on his back and sank its teeth into his shoulder. Before he had a chance to react the creature flew off and smashed into the railings of the vessel. The old Helmsman stood holding the remnants of the cabin stool in his hand.

Var looked about the boat. The sea was churning with black bodies.

"Quickly!" yelled Var. Gero leapt for the ladder and hauled his bulk nimbly onto the roof. He turned leaned over the edge and grabbed Jed's collar. He unceremoniously lifted the old Helmsman off the deck. Through the heavy rain they could see more and more of the black beasts leaping onto the deck.

"Don't we have any weapons?" asked Lin desperately.

"They are below in the cabin" snorted Gero wrapping a torn piece of cloth around the wounds on his arm. Var had uncovered the mounted nail gun and was frantically trying to urge the rusting weapon into life.

"Does that thing work?" asked Gero.

"We'll soon see" shouted Var. He kicked the gun's compressor for a second time. This time it whistled into action. Var drew back the arming bolt and aimed the weapon at the oncoming tide of creatures. He squeezed the trigger and the compressed air hissed as it shot out its spiked metal payload. Var kept his finger firmly on the trigger and aimed the gun strafing it across the deck. The metal shards tore through the kekken felling them in droves. As each one fell another snarling beast took its place.

The gun finally gave out, the empty clicking sound indicating it was out of ammunition. The others had scoured the top deck for anything resembling a weapon. Lin had both her knives drawn, Gero was wielding the boats anchor and Jed had found a rusty short sword.

The creatures swarmed over the deck and began to surround the cabin and climb.

"There are so many" said Lin in defeat.

"We're not done yet" growled Gero turning on the terrified tribeswoman. Jed put his hand on his daughter's arm.

"Never give up" said the old man. Before any of them could react the aging Helmsman screamed a blood curdling battle cry and leapt from the deck into the seething mass of black bodies. He slashed about him wildly, possessed by rage, he hacked and stabbed as the creatures surrounded him.

"Father!" screamed Lin. The old man's body was lost beneath the hideous sea of animals. Lin dropped to her knees. Var turned and grabbed her by the arms.

"Not now!" he hollered at her. "There will be time for mourning later." The sadness had already overwhelmed her. Var slapped her across the face.

"Lin, we need you now" he pleaded. Anger flared in the young woman's eyes and she shook off his grasp. Var turned to see Gero swiping a creature from the boat with the anchor. The dead beast landed some distance from the boat. As Var watched the creature hit the surface he noticed something else in the water. His attention was torn as he felt his false leg jerk. A kekken had crested the top deck and slashed out, clawing through his trousers.

"You're too late" hissed Var. He brought his leg up and stamped into the face of the creature. The heavy metal foot stove in the kekken's head and it fell backward into its brothers. Var looked out to the side once more. The ocean was still full of black bodies but many of them were now floating lifelessly on the surface. The waters around the sea blade were in turmoil like some deathly tempest whipping them to its will. Then Var noticed a large creature landing on the lower deck. It hissed and clicked at the retreating animals around it. With blistering speed it slashed and severed its own kind. More kekken hurdled in behind it and within moments the new arrivals had killed everything in sight.

The tall creature climbed over the piles of bodies towards the cabin. It looked up at the shocked

survivors. It moved its arm and signed.

<<Friend>>

"You can't trust it" shouted Lin understanding the movement.

"This one I have met before" said Var calmly. Gero cast him a look of caution. "It's OK my friend, I know what I am doing."

"That'll be a first" grumbled the giant.

Var slowly climbed down the ladder trying not slip on the blood and entrails that sloshed about the lower deck. He stood before the creature. He could clearly see his reflection in its black eyes and smell the fetid stench of its breath. Var held out his arms towards the creature and turned his palms upwards.

The creature placed a talon on each of Var's wrists. The young warrior's head jerked back as he linked minds with the sea creature.

[I had feared we were too late] the thought hammered into Var's mind. He had bonded with these creatures before but he had forgotten how disturbing it was.

[What happened?] questioned Var.

[Our world dies. The oceans freeze. Some of our kind believe the prophecy is flawed or at least misread]

[I don't understand] thought Var.

[Our meeting many seasons ago was not chance. We believe it is you who can save our world from its icy death. That is why we helped you. Things are moving much quicker than we expected, it is now time for you to act]

[Act. I have no idea what you are talking about. If I am to save this world I do not know how]

[We have uncovered an ancient gate. It lies near the Pillars of Itna. We believe it is the gateway to the gods. Only the chosen can open it. You are the chosen. You must open the gate and go before the gods, persuade them that this world is worth saving]

Var gathered his thoughts.

[Then you must take me there] stated Var.

[We will, but you must first find the key]

[I knew it wouldn't be that simple. Where is the key?]

[If we knew then we would have obtained it. Only you will know it. You must hurry; the number of my brothers that are turning is quickly growing]

[You mean the ones that attacked us?]

[Yes. They too can see the forever darkness approaching, but they believe that opening the great gate will anger the gods and seal our fate. They will do what they can to stop you]

[What if they are right?] The thought sprang unbidden into Var's mind.

[Then we will all meet the darkness together]

Var staggered backwards as the mind link was broken. The creature blinked its filmy eyelids and disappeared over the side. Gero appeared next to Var and steadied him.

"What did it say?" he questioned.

"I need to speak with your father" replied Var. "It looks like our vacation is over." Var gave his friend a grim smile.

Chapter 3 - The Merthurian

Titan Lothair sat motionless on his throne, his head supported by his right hand. He stared unblinking at the pitted stone tiles oblivious to the noise and mayhem that surrounded him. The court of the Magta had not seen this much disturbance since the days of the first migration. The ancient race of giants, despite their sizeable presence in the world had always chosen to live a life of solitude away from the other races of Gebshu. It was this choice that was now being furiously debated.

The court was housed in a high vaulted chamber, with tiered seats facing each other across a narrow open area. At the end of this corridor on top of a dais carved from a single piece of stone sat the Titan. The court operated in a very simple manner. The Titan would stand and announce the issue at hand, and then open the debate to the court. Individuals would stand and state their opinion. As the debate continued the assembled Magta would make their decision and move to the side of the court where they agreed with the argument being put forward. After only a short time the two sides of the court opposed each other. The debate would continue until the Titan would stand and declare it over. The clerk of the court then counted the members on each side. The side with the most, won the argument and the Titan would then pass judgement accordingly.

The two sides of the court were already clearly split, albeit unevenly. The priest Sabine had been listening to those alongside him trying to make their case, and had quickly seen the bodies around him desert to the other side. He clenched his fist around his walking stick and used it as a brace to lift his aging frame from his seat. As the elder priest steadily rose to his feet the commotion quelled. For the first time since the debate began Titan Lothair lifted his eyes.

"Gentleman" started Sabine. "I have listened to your views and the case you make is strong, of that there is no doubt. You speak from the heart and your intentions are sincere. However they are misguided." The opposing throng started a low murmur. Sabine continued.

"You all know our history, and the reasons we removed ourselves from the world. Those reasons have not changed. You now seek to move our civilisation back into the world of the Dumon, because life has become difficult." The priest straightened his back as best he could and thumped his stick into the floor. "Do not be weak my friends, you must keep the faith. Our spiritual Master has already spoken on this matter and he has seen our future. Our future is here in the Fortress of Ages."

One of the warrior caste sat opposite the priest got to his feet. The giants surrounding him all silently urging the response they were all thinking.

"Even if that means the extinction of our people?"

This was the question they had all wanted to ask, but before Sabine had a chance to answer the colossal doors to the court chamber creaked open. The gathered throng turned and watched as the Hagon, the Master of the Shining Caste slowly made his way into hall.

He shuffled between the two sides casting a quick sideways glance at Sabine as he passed. He stopped before the dais. He struggled to lift his head up as his crooked back held it back. He was as old as the stone upon which he stood. He had guided the Magta in their spiritual needs for longer than any could remember. His visions of the future had kept the mighty giants locked away from the world.

"My Lord, please forgive my tardiness, these old bones are not as fast as they once were." Lothair smiled and stood.

"I think in truth we have all been waiting for your wisdom and guidance, please..." and the Titan gestured to the floor. Hagon turned and flicked the fur cloak away from his shoulders the remaining flecks of snow swirling in the air. There was a deliberate silence before the old Master spoke.

"Brothers and Sisters please hear my words." Despite his years, the master priest's voice boomed around the chamber, he was an accomplished orator and the passion in his blue eyes burned as he took the stage.

"Many moons ago the remainder of our people moved here and built this great fortress. The world around was descending into chaos and we wanted no part of the Dumon disease. This was all foreseen by my forebears and their guidance saved our people from extinction as the Gods cleansed the planet. We have lived here in peace ever since. I have seen our future. Our future is here."

A look of disappointment crept across the face of the Titan.

"We have endured hardships before, and even though the snow and ice now claw at our walls we will prevail. It is the will of the gods that we remain here and see out our destiny."

Konrad, the warrior that had spoken against Sabine, once again stood.

"I respect your words and visions Master Hagon, but staying in the fortress will be certain death for many of our people, the young and the old will not survive the next winter. We have endured cruel winters before, but last year the snow never left our gates all season. It is yet worse this season. Surely the Gods would not condemn us to a frozen fate?"

The aging priest made his way to stand before the giant warrior.

"Young Konrad, it is not your place to question the will of the Gods. You have always been keen to leave this place, to make your mark on the world, perhaps now you are using our situation as an excuse to follow your own dreams?"

"Do I have dreams of life outside these walls?" barked Konrad "Of course I do old man, I am Magta. I have not forgotten who I am." The Titan rose quickly to his feet and held out his hand towards the young warrior.

"Remember your place young Konrad" said Lothair. The warrior drew a deep breath, momentarily ashamed of his outburst and nodded towards the Titan. He looked at Hagon, trying to read his emotionless features.

"My apologies Master" he said quietly.

"We are all Magta" replied Hagon. "Our future has been decided. If it is the Gods' will that remaining here will mean the end of our people, then this is how we see our end of days."

Silence echoed around the chamber.

The heavy atmosphere was broken at last as Dagmar one of the Forged Caste stood and coughed.

"If I may speak?" he directed his question towards Lothair purposely avoiding the gaze of the master priest. Dagmar didn't wait for a response from the Titan.

"It is true we are guided by the Gods but this court is governed by law. This is a matter of law not faith. All those present should decide and take their seats." With this the rugged blacksmith took his seat. Noise once again erupted from the court. The Titan held out both arms to quell the commotion. The opening he had looked for had now presented itself. The side of the court that opposed Hagon and Sabine was in the ascendancy. He would follow the law and call for a count, he had wanted to move his people seasons ago but even he dared not challenge the Shining Caste.

"Dagmar has spoken the truth. You will now choose a side and take your seats." Lothair held the murderous gaze from Hagon. The old priest looked away in disgust and moved to climb the steps. As he moved sideways to join Sabine an older warrior held his elbow to steady him.

"Let me help you Master." As Hagon turned he saw the seats on his side of the house filling as the Magta flooded across. He sat and smiled. He knew that the majority would follow him. Faith amongst the people was still strong. He looked at Lothair, raising his eyebrows.

Lothair had underestimated the power of Hagon, he had hoped common sense or even a sense of self preservation would have prevailed. As he looked out on the clear result his heart sagged.

"The result is clear for all to see" said the Titan. "However it is my right as the lawful ruler of this court." He was cut off mid sentence as Hagon shouted.

"You must obey the decision! You are not above the law!"

Lothair said nothing; he waited for Hagon to take his seat.

"The decision will be upheld. The Magta will remain." He glared at Hagon. "In order to ensure the survival of our race, I would call for volunteers who would travel to the outside world to find and bring back food and supplies. So is my ruling."

Lothair and Hagon both knew he had just given a free pass to all those who wanted to leave.

"And you my Lord?" questioned Hagon. "Will you volunteer? Or will you remain with your people?"

"I will do what is right" replied the Titan.

*

Lothair pulled his grey fur cloak tightly around his shoulders. He leaned forward and placed his hands on the snow covered crenellations high up on the fortress wall. A long line of people stretched out into the distance like a dark scar in the landscape. Some pulled carts whilst others carried what belongings they could on their backs. They were making their way to the fleet of ships moored at the end of the peninsular. Their own harbour had frozen solid last season and showed no signs of thawing even now during the summer months. His sad musings were pierced by the thought that at least some of his people had a chance of survival. Too few, he thought, far too few. Not for the first time during his reign he questioned his ability to lead his people.

*

Emmerick had been watching the migration with some confusion. He had heard the outcome of the debate, and he was more than happy with the decision to remain in the Fortress. So he could not understand why so many people were now leaving. He had been busy in the Grand Archive when he had heard the commotion outside. At first he thought he had been found out and quickly rushed to the window. As he rubbed away the frost on the window he saw the long line of people making their way out of the main gate. He breathed a sigh of relief.

The Grand Archive was the museum of the Magta. All of their great treasures were stored there. Emmerick worked under the strict supervision of the Archive Master - Markus. Markus had guarded and cared for the antiquities since the building of the fortress. His eyesight was now failing so five seasons ago he had appointed Emmerick as his assistant.

The young giant had been awestruck by the contents of the archive. The grand jewels of previous Titans, the ancient books documenting his people's histories but most intriguing of all were the hand crafted weapons. These unique masterpieces were of untold age, and each had its own special properties. Even Lothair's great war maul now resided in the archive. The enormous hammer took pride of place in the public display. Secured behind its glass case the maul was a symbol of power to the Magta. Emmerick thought it was a shame that such things of beauty and function were kept locked away.

Over time Markus had slowly left his assistant to get on with the day to day tasks in the archive. One of Emmerick's tasks was to work his way through the vast weapon archive that wasn't part of the public display. This part of the archive held many of the lesser weapons, that either had not been wielded by the more famous warriors, or had less or even unknown power. Nonetheless they were still all of considerable value, which fortunately for Emmerick had saved his life.

The young apprentice had been meticulously cleaning a small jewelled knife. He held it in his hand admiring its beauty. He had run his finger gently along the blade, and only this slightest touch had drawn blood. He then turned the knife and ran the edge against his workbench. The dagger cut into the wooden bench as if it were butter. Emmerick was enamoured by the weapon so much so that he had convinced himself that Markus would not notice if it went missing.

That evening he had gone out onto the sea ice with his bow hunting for vayleg. Vayleg were small birds that lived mainly in the water but came out occasionally onto the ice to sleep and breed. They were easy targets on the pack ice and had become the staple diet of the Magta. On this evening Emmerick had found himself much further out than normal, and there was still no sign of any prey.

The darkness had started to pull in and Emmerick was now thinking of returning to the Fortress. He didn't want to go empty handed, but he certainly didn't want to be out on the sea ice at night. Despite his vast bulk and muscular physique the rumours that spread like a plague through the fortress were more than enough to make him wary.

As he crouched low in the snow scanning the horizon for signs of a target he heard a crunch in the crisp snow behind him. He heard a whirring sound. He stood and turned and saw two small figures approach him at speed. He was about to stand his ground when the whirring sound increased and a spinning bolas appeared from the gloom wrapping itself around his legs. Before he could react the first man leapt at him. He thundered into the giant's chest knocking him into the snow with a soft thwump.

Emmerick tried to scrabble backwards across the ice desperate to regain his footing. As he struggled the small jewelled knife he had taken from the archive fell from his jacket into the snow. The two men stopped and looked at the treasure framed on the white canvas. Emmerick recognised the covetous look in their bearded faces.

"It's yours if you want it" stammered Emmerick. The men glanced at each other and then laughed simultaneously. The larger of the two men stepped forward and picked up the knife. He then took a step closer to Emmerick. His head came up to the giant's chest. Despite the difference in size, it was clear who had the upper hand.

"We'll take what we want ogre, we don't need your permission." grunted the man.

"Of course" replied Emmerick quickly. "But there are more like it, I can get you more."

The man drew the knife. It resembled a short sword in the man's grip.

"Why would we want an ogre trinket?" said the main tilting his head as if feigning interest.

"It's no ordinary blade" continued the desperate Emmerick. "The edge will cut through anything." The men looked sceptical. "Try it!" insisted the giant.

"Maybe I will" snarled the warrior as he held the knife up towards the giant's throat. Emmerick tried to move his head as far away from the blade as possible. The small man crouched and brought the knife down with one swift movement. The dagger cut through the wire bolas and buried itself deep into the ice. The warrior looked up surprised at the giant. He stood and withdrew a small sword that was hung at his waist. He sliced the knife across his sword blade. The tip of his sword dropped into the snow.

"Gesh!" exclaimed the warrior. The other man stepped forward and picked up the sword tip.

"How many more like this?" he said thrusting the metal shard towards the giant.

"They are not all exactly the same." started Emmerick nervously "But they are all hand crafted weapons, each with its own unique property." He flashed a glance between the two men, trying to gauge their next move. They leant their heads together closely and whispered to each other. The second warrior quickly turned and ran back into the darkness. A short while later he returned dragging something behind him on a crude sled. As he got closer Emmerick could see it was piled high with huge strips of flesh. It had been some time since the giant had seen so much food.

"You bring us magic weapons, we will give you food?" It was a simple trade thought Emmerick quickly realising that not only could he get out of this with his life but he could turn this to his advantage. Food had been rationed in the Fortress since the onset of permanent winter. This much food could get him whatever he wanted.

"How will I find you?" asked Emmerick. The first warrior stepped forward and removed a small green disk that hung around his neck. He handed it to the giant.

"Wear this, and we will find you." stated the man. "You have two moons. Do not break our bargain, or we will come and take what you owe us". Without another word the two warriors turned and disappeared into the darkness. Emmerick reached down and untangled the remains of the bolas from around his feet. He threw it into the snow. He felt guilty; he had just bargained his way out of a fight. A true Magta would have fought to the death. Then he looked again at the sled piled high with meat, and he smiled as he grabbed the rope.

*

Even with the crowded streets, Emmerick was still cautious. His cover story had been surprisingly robust. He had told his family that he had found patchy details in the Archive about an effective method of fishing through the ice. Perhaps it was because the people were simply grateful to have real food that they didn't care where it came from. Whatever the reason, he was careful not to reveal his secret. He had met with the Merthurian warriors many times since their first dramatic encounter and they had been true to their word and delivered a bounty of food each time. At first he had only taken the smaller items from the archive, but as time passed he wanted to impress his new found friends and so he smuggled more and more impressive items.

On this occasion he had taken two magnificent arm scythes. The small blades were attached to a brace which was strapped around the forearm, with the blade following the length of the arm back towards the elbow. A sudden arm movement in a downward direction would cause the blade to swing out in a vicious arc. The blade could be retracted in the same way. What made these weapons special was apparently their ability to pre-empt an attack. Emmerick wasn't quite sure what this meant but he knew that the Merthurian would be suitably impressed.

He cast one last glance back towards the rocky mountain on which sat the Fortress of Ages. There was no-one following him. One advantage of the icy weather was that you could easily spot someone in the monotonous landscape, unless there was a storm.

Each time he had walked out into the frozen tundra, he had no idea when the Merthurian would contact him. He had become prepared and was slowly learning how to cope with the plummeting temperatures and terrain. He wore fur trousers and animal skin boots onto which he had fashioned wooden skids. The skids spread his weight and enabled him to move faster across the ice. He wore many layers of clothes all wrapped up in a massive fur cloak. His was covered with a fur hat which he tied beneath his chin. Slung across his back was another large fur roll, wound around a single wooden pole. For the first time he now also sported a woollen cloth which he had tied around his face keeping his mouth and nose covered. The ice now formed on the outside of the wool where his warm breath met the cold air. The crude sled he had first used was tied to his left leg and now moved in spurts across the snow.

He had been walking for some time now and despite his effective equipment the cold wind was starting to bite at his flesh. He looked up trying to gauge the location of Shu and determine the time. Dark clouds surrounded the giant. He swore and looked back at his tracks in the snow. It was too far to go back now.

He took the fur roll off his back and withdrew the pole. He rammed the pointed stick into the ground. He then unrolled the large full blanket and placed it over the wooden pole. He moved quickly around the edge of the blanket piling the snow up and then stamping it down. The wind was picking up and the snow was gradually working its way up the fur tent. He opened the flap and hurried inside the makeshift shelter. The relief at being out of the wind was profound. He relaxed and pulled the fur blanket to close the gap. There was just enough room to sit upright. Next time I'll bring something to sit on he thought to himself as the cold ground made him shiver.

Inside the tent Emmerick watched mesmerised as the slivers of light that shone through a few small holes slowly lost their strength and the darkness enveloped the scene. Emmerick put his head into his chest and pulled his legs in close and closed his eyes.

He awoke with a violent start, for an instance forgetting where he was. Light was once again piercing his shelter. The he heard it again the sound that had originally woken him. A loud guttural growl. He quickly tried to open the tent flap, but the snow had piled up. It took some effort to lift the weight of the snow as he emerged into the blinding landscape. As he staggered to his feet he stopped dead in his tracks as if he had become part of his frozen surroundings. In front of him was an enormous animal.

The white furred animal had four powerful legs, each paw sporting long black talons. At the end of its stocky neck was a streamline head, dark black eyes and two massive downward pointing fangs. The animal flexed its considerable neck muscles and opened its mouth making a hideous growl. Emmerick could see razor sharp teeth lining its maw. The animal snorted, and for the first time the frightened giant realised that there was a warrior sat upon the back of the beast.

"He is a Shektar and don't worry he won't bite.... unless I ask him to" grinned the rider. The rider sat behind the animal's two front legs on a leather saddle with what looked like reigns around the creature's neck. The rider patted the animal's shoulder lovingly and lent forward whispering in the beast's short stubby ears. The massive beast bent its legs and settled onto the ice. The rider vaulted off with consummate ease.

"So you are the thieving ogre" said the rider staring at the still unmoving Emmerick.

"I, I, I suppose I am" stammered the giant.

"I am Tol Son Ray" said the rider.

"My name is Emmerick" he said re-gaining some composure. "Is Aron not coming? I was expecting Aron."

"Aron is busy, besides I wanted to meet you for myself. I have seen your kind only from a distance. You are indeed as massive as my scouts tell me."

"Are you the leader?" questioned the giant.

"Of sorts" replied Toll Son Ray. "Tell me Em-mer -ick, how many of you are there in that mountain fortress of yours?" The rider gestured back over his shoulder. Emmerick was surprised by the question.

"Not as many as there once -were" he replied vaguely. "Over a third of our number are leaving even as we speak."

"Interesting" said Toll Son Ray scratching his long black beard. "Anyway I digress, back to business, what have you brought for me this time?" Emmerick was keen to show his worth and un-clicked his cloak and let it fall to the ground. As he did the sudden movement spooked the animal and it raised itself up on to all fours growling at the source of its irritation. The giant jumped back. At this point he noticed that apart from the rider and the beast there was no sign of anything else - no food. He stared into the rider's icy blue gaze and clearly understood his intentions.

Toll Son Ray leapt towards the giant unsheathing a curved blade as he did so. Emmerick was no warrior and he reacted by bringing his arms up to cover his face. As he did the long curved blade of the arm scythe shot out blocking the attack. Emmerick drew away from his attacker and in doing so the blade swung back this time the tip slicing across his sword hand. Toll Son Ray cursed as he dropped his sword into the snow.

The huge Shektar howled as if also wounded and turned to face the giant. Emmerick slowly moved backwards as the massive animal padded towards him, saliva dripping from its mouth. The creature launched itself and once more the helpless giant reacted. The razor sharp scythe tore through the animal's neck killing it instantly, its forward motion carrying it into Emmerick.

Toll Son Ray had retrieved his sword and was now walking towards the pinned giant. Emmerick kicked and struggled trying to free his legs from under the dead weight. He freed his left leg but it was too late the rider was on him. Toll Son Ray did not even look at Emmerick. The Giant could clearly see tears streaming down his face, as the warrior knelt down beside the fallen animal. He rested his head on the dead beast's fur and slowly stroked it whilst whispering gently as if soothing a small child.

Emmerick wasted no time he kicked once more and freed his leg. He got to his feet and ran. He kept looking over his shoulder expecting to see the warrior in pursuit. Every time he looked back the small figure remained crouched over the fallen animal. After a lung burning trek the outline of the fortress loomed into view and Emmerick sighed with relief, although it did not stop the sickness in the pit of his stomach. He knew this was far from over.

*

Emmerick rubbed his eyes; they stung due to his lack of sleep. Pouring over the ancient records in the Archive wasn't helping but he was desperate to find out more about the Merthurian. Coupled with these worries Markus had been around asking questions and generally taking a more active role. It was only a matter of time before he discovered the dozens of missing artefacts.

He had exhausted all of the older texts, none of them had any reference to the warriors he had encountered. He had then gone over the more recent historical books but still nothing. He grabbed his cloak and wrapped it tightly around his shoulders. He opened the side door to the Archive and carefully locked it behind him. The cold wind tore at his face and he pulled the cloak further around covering all but his eyes.

He made the slippery descent down the main street and out through the fortress gate. After a short while he made it to the old harbour. The two huge stone walls that once protruded out into the ocean were now completed encrusted with ice. The once busy port was now eerily quiet. The only sign of life was a pale glow coming from the windows of houses surrounding the harbour.

If he was going to find anyone who knew about the Merthurian then one of the elders who lived here was his best hope. He knocked on the first door. He waited patiently. There was no sound from within. He knocked once more, not wanting to cause offence. This time he heard the scrape of wood on stone, so he stepped back and waited. The door slowly opened and an aging giant peered around.

"Yes?" said the old man.

"I am sorry to bother you, but I am Emmerick from the Archive. I was hoping to speak to someone about the Dumon warriors that live out on the ice sheet." replied Emmerick politely.

"What for?" asked the old giant.

"To update the histories of the Archive. We try and keep current events recorded and there seems to be a gap where these people are concerned. We would happily credit you with the research."

The old giant opened the door.

"Best come in then" and he gestured for Emmerick to enter.

The giant retrieved a chair from his kitchen and sat it opposite his own in front of a small fire. He pointed at it, and Emmerick sat down.

"What is it you want to know?" he started.

"Firstly your name" replied Emmerick.

"I am Eskil, son of Berg. I have been a fisherman here for..." Eskil scratched his chin and looked up thoughtfully.

"Forever" he concluded. He laughed and then the laugh turned into a cough.

"So you have met the Merthurian?" enquired Emmerick impatiently.

"A couple of times, many years ago of course, it has been a while since I have been out of this hut. I was fishing along the edge of the sea ice, when it was much further back than it is now. I was hauling in my nets when I noticed something thrashing about. As I hauled it in I could see it was a Dumon, one of those underwater ones. He had a mask over his mouth and face, a strange looking fellow. He had his arm trapped in my net, obviously trying to grab himself a free meal."

Eskil coughed again and stared blankly at his guest.

"Please continue" insisted Emmerick.

"Ah yes. Of course" replied Eskil seeming to return to his mind. "I freed his arm and offered him the fish. He was very grateful and we sat and chatted for a while. Apparently they had abandoned their home on the ocean floor and had made a new one out on the sea ice. It seemed a bit farfetched, as nothing could really live out in those conditions. He told me they still dived underwater to gather food and resources but the temperatures had dropped and they could only spend a short amount of time beneath the surface."

"Did he say anything about how many of them there were, or mention anything about animals that they rode?" asked Emmerick.

"Let me think now, no I don't think so, nothing about numbers anyway. He did say something about some kind of animal - a shep something."

"Shektar" interrupted the younger giant. Eskil narrowed his eyes at his guest.

"Yes, that's it. Shektar." He stared hard at Emmerick, but the reason behind his surprise slowly faded and he returned to his story. "As I was saying, the Mer, that's my name for them, are paired when children with these animals. Apparently they grow up together and form some kind of life long bond. All sounded a bit sketchy to me." Emmerick had gone very pale. "Are you feeling OK?"

"Yes I am fine" he replied quietly. "What else do you know about them?"

"That's it really. I saw them a few times after that but only from a distance." Emmerick stood up to leave.

"My thanks to you Eskil and the thanks of the archive, you have been very helpful." He pulled his cloak on.

"You are welcome to stay, I have some broth on the stove" The old giant seemed to have a hint of desperation in his voice.

"That's very kind Eskil, but I have to be getting back."

"Of course" replied the elder giant.

Emmerick hurried up the steep slope toward the fortress, his mind swimming. He was now even more worried than he had been before. His time for concern about the Mer was short lived. At the main gate, flanked by two city guards, stood a very stern looking Markus.

Chapter 4 - The Red Gate

The weak light of the fading star silently crept its way across the landscape extinguishing the darkness. As the shadows withdrew they revealed the army of the new Emperor spreading out across the head of the valley.

Lord Vas had moved his forces during the night bypassing the town of Watco-Tun. He'd gambled that the human shield had been a delaying tactic by the renegade Virtues. He had led his men through the narrowing valley and they now prepared to lay siege to the vast temple of Tetra-Mor. The ancient building housed the central administration of the recently deceased Virtue of Fire.

The mist was slowly lifting from the valley floor but it still clung to the higher reaches of the foothills of the Mountain of Voice. At the end of the valley the landscape rose violently into sheer cliff faces. The temple of Tetra-Mor had been carved into the rock, and its interior burrowed deep into the extinct volcano. Originally a place of pilgrimage for all of the Dumonii, it had become the seat of power for the Virtue of Fire.

Thousands of steps swayed left and right cutting a precarious pathway to the temple. Carved entirely from the rock face, five gargantuan pillars marked the entrance, completely dwarfing the intricately carved doorway which led inside the mountain. Above the pillars were carved various reliefs depicting battles of long dead Virtues. They surrounded the central motif of Shu. Over millennia the temple had spread across the rock with carvings, steps, pillars, terraces and openings peppering the stone like a living organism. To the far left of the temple the waters from high up in the mountains cascaded over the cliff. The waterfall provided the only movement in the otherwise lifeless diorama.

At the foot of the cliff a small town had grown up to provide for the temple. The enclave was protected by a formidable wall which stretched all the way across the valley forming an unbreakable defensive line. The massive structure was punctuated by the Red Gate. The fortified twin towers of the Red Gate rose out of the wall standing guard over the only entrance. The Emperor looked at the obstacle before him. The gate had originally been given its name because of the crimson coloured sandstone from which it was built. As legends and tales grew its name had become a homage to those who had died at its feet, spilling their blood on the impenetrable blockade. As each Virtue placed their stamp on the temple the two towers had been heightened in several stages. The top two tiers shone in the morning light in brilliant contrast to the dull sandstone. The skulls of the fallen had been embedded into the fabric of the buildings. The macabre structure stood defiant.

The legions of the Emperor were well drilled and they had fanned out before the wall, making sure to keep at a safe distance from the defending archers. Shouting at the rear of his forces grabbed the Emperor's attention. A lone Reaver was running, colliding with his comrades as he came rushing towards Lord Vas. He could see blood running down the man's arm and dripping from his fingers. Several bolt gun spikes extended from his ceramic armour.

"Make way!" bellowed the Emperor. The exhausted soldier collapsed on his knees. He attempted a feeble salute.

"My Lord" he gasped.

"Get this man some water" commanded Lord Vas. A Dominator handed him a water flask and Vas knelt to give the wounded man a drink.

"Thank you my Lord" he coughed. "I am Mor-Te. I was part of the rear guard you posted." The soldier paused looking into the black orbs of the Emperor with clear apprehension. "The town was not empty" he said at last. "A massive army was hidden there and it is now on the way up the valley. We were spotted by their scouts. The rest of the squad bought me time to bring you this message."

Lord Vas had realised his mistake the moment he had seen the Reaver bump his way into camp. There would be time to reflect on this later. This new enemy would trap his men between them and the Red Gate. It would be a massacre. He had been confident that he could lay siege to the Gate, but that would take time. The ground beneath his feet started to vibrate gently.

"We don't have much time" He said, almost to himself. He looked down at the panting soldier. "Thank you Mor-Te. You and your squad have saved many lives with your sacrifice." The Emperor drew himself up mustering every ounce of confidence. "Dominators to me!" he yelled.

The twelve Dominators that were the personal bodyguard of the Emperor sprang into life and were instantly in attendance to their Lord. They held the same status as the Principles and were handpicked from the very best that the Dumonii had to offer. An elite guard. Each man was a veteran soldier and accomplished warrior, fiercely proud to hold the position of a Dominator. They took orders only from the Emperor. Lord Vas surveyed the stony faces of his retinue, not even a flicker of fear in their eyes.

Vas quickly relayed his orders to his men. They grinned as he explained his tactics. He may not have been the best tactician but when it came down to a fight he was unmatched. The Dominators nodded their approval and hurried to organise the troops.

*

The former Principle to the deceased Virtue of Fire stood leaning on the crenulated battlements of the left tower. Fi-Ota had served the Virtue for as long as he could remember, the news of his mentor's death at the hand of the new Emperor had been hard to hear. His grief was short lived when the Virtues of Air and Earth had suggested he take the mantel and become the new Virtue of Fire. This was normally an appointment made by the Emperor, but in these current circumstances the short balding man was more than happy to accept the honour. Fi-Aka as he was now known interlocked his fingers and bent them back clicking the joints.

"This will be a great day for the Virtues" he said as he aimlessly stroked his beard. "I hope we get in on the action, I don't want to sit up here all day and watch the other Virtues take all the glory."

His own replacement was in attendance.

"I am sure there will be time for you to join the fray my Lord" said Sho-Ota. Patience was not a known trait of those born in the shadow of the Mountain of Voice.

"We will watch as their bodies crash against the Red Gate, and then we will descend upon them like a devastating torrent of lava flowing from our ancient mountain." snarled the Virtue of Fire as he raised his arms into the air. Principle Sho-Ota stifled a chuckle. He had known Fi for many revolutions. He was not known for his rhetoric. In fact Sho-Ota had been completely surprised at his appointment. An efficient Principle he had been. He was an accomplished administrator but he was certainly no leader. It was common practice for anyone wishing a position to fight in the ring for the honour. Under those circumstances Sho-Ota was confident he would now be in charge. He looked deridingly at the would-be Virtue lording himself over the men.

"I'll get my chance" he thought.

Sho-Ota looked out on the massing ranks of the Emperor's men. He felt a tiny pang of guilt. Slaughtering the Emperor and his men like this was nothing to be proud of.

*

The ranks of aging vehicles coughed and spluttered into life as the Emperor moved by. Thick black smoke poured from the twin exhausts of the grounders. They worked more thanks to luck than anything else. The Dumonii had once been a civilisation that had embraced technology and they accomplished much through study and research. Those times had long since evaporated and the left-overs from that age now steadily rusted as did the knowledge of their upkeep.

Lord Vas had quickly realised this and had extended the hand of the Emperor to all the skilled Replicators, Medicators and Servitors that remained. Their renewed enthusiasm was the only reason that Vas had the fleet of vehicles that now rumbled towards the Red Gate.

The Emperor could feel the ground vibrate and he knew that it wasn't caused by his vehicles. The formidable army of the Virtue's of Air and Earth now bore up the valley eager to crush their prey.

Vas hammered his hand against the rear door of the nearby grounder. The heavy metal door swung open and the Emperor squeezed his muscular frame into the compartment. The majority of the grounders had been designed as troop carriers, each one able to take between five and eight men. There were also several variations, some had a large bolt gun mounted above the driver, a few had no crew chamber but instead were designed to carry equipment and supplies and came with a crane arm behind the cab. There were also two other variations. The Replicators had explained to the Emperor that they had been used for crossing small rivers or gullies. They had large flat metal tread plates that could be unfolded to create a temporary road way above the vehicle. They each had extended exhausts and breather snorkels to enable them to work in deep water. All of the Emperor's plans now relied on these creaking vehicles.

The lead grounder barked as the driver accelerated towards the left side of the great wall. Despite their problems, when working they could achieve an acceptable speed. The two bridge layer variations tried to keep pace close behind. As it came within range of the wall the bolt gun opened fire.

The long range weapons of the Dumonii were restricted to compressed air bolt guns, crossbows and bows. They had no stable explosive compound. A mixture of chemicals was occasionally used for mining, but it was so delicate it had limited use in warfare. Early experiments had resulted in more loss of life for those using the explosive rather than the enemy forces. After the initial salvo's of spikes and bolts most Dumonii combat was settled hand to hand, and face to face.

As the first grounder bounded over the rough ground the metal bolts ricocheted off the sandstone and most sailed harmlessly over the wall. The defenders had been prepared for a vehicular assault and large catapults fired round clay pots high into the air. They were swiftly followed by a volley of flaming arrows.

As the pots smashed around the advancing column the arrows set the sticky liquid inside on fire. The smoke from the armoured carriers now mixed with the burning grass and a sea of intoxicating vapour slowly enveloped the battlefield. Several vehicles had been hit and were still travelling at speed burning as they hurtled forward, the rushing air fanning the flames. Despite their fiery onslaught the soldiers on top of the wall could not slow the mechanical advance.

The lead vehicle crested the small bank only a short way from the main wall. Its speed made it leave the ground and it landed hard before smashing through a wooden boundary fence. As it approached the wall the driver pulled hard on the steering lever. The left track froze and the grounder lurched violently in that direction. The Virtue's men now pelted the attackers by hand with the flammable pots. As it pulled away the lead carrier was completely engulfed in flames.

The two awkward looking machines were next to clear the bank. Their bridge equipment was in full extend and the hydraulic rams hissed under the strain of movement. The two crates thundered into the great wall. The shock waves sent those on top flying. Despite their speed they had made little impact on the colossal obstacle. Their bridge ramps however now extended to just beneath the stone crenellations. With horror the new Virtue of Fire saw the simple plan unfolding.

The next grounder hammered up the artificial ramp and smashed through the top of the wall. Stone exploded in all directions as the vehicle crashed through and plummeted into the houses behind. A second grounder followed suit, its greater speed sending it pounding through the roofs of the previously protected town. The tracks fragmented as it fell and the metal and stone hellstorm pummelled the defending soldiers. Chaos ensued as the Virtue of Fire's Missionrai struggled to keep a semblance of order.

The grounders now climbing the burning ramp had slowed and when reaching the summit now turned to drive along the top of the wall in both directions. The defending soldiers ran for their lives as the wide tracks demolished the top of the walls and left no hiding place. Some jumped to avoid being pulverised by the rampaging vehicles. Several of the personnel carriers had not made the sharp turn on top of the wall and had tumbled into the narrow street behind. The dazed but organised men were quickly at the task of securing their advantage.

The Emperor's forces poured through the forced opening soon filling the breach themselves. The ground troops now ran attempting to reach the man made ramp, trying to avoid the black shower of arrows peppering them from the advancing force from behind. Those already atop the wall now lay down covering fire for their fleeing brothers. The Emperor threw open the metal door and was met immediately by a black armoured entourage of Dominators.

"It goes well my Lord" said Oma-Sem constantly checking about him for any signs of danger.

"Leave the majority of troops on the wall. We must defend against the larger army coming up the valley. We must ensure the Red Gate stays closed. We will be in the same position if the Virtues manage to get their men through the gate and cut us off." The Emperor didn't wait for a response instead he had jumped onto a sloping roof below. His weight cracking the weathered tiles. He was followed closely by his faithful bodyguard. Lord Vas stooped and grabbed the metal guttering of the building using it to slow his descent into the cobbled street below. As he lowered himself the fixings holding the channelling faltered and as Lord Vas landed debris from the building rained down around him.

He drew the two war hammers that were secured to the back plate of his armour seeming unaffected by the turmoil around him. The weapons extended and the heads rotated ninety degrees clicking into place. He raced along the narrow street towards the Red Gate. He swiftly side-stepped a body falling from the battle above. It thudded into the cobbles. The scene ahead was one of total devastation. The area where the two spearhead grounders had cleared the main wall was a mass of rubble and burning timber. The Emperor's men had secured their position at either side of the street and above on the wall. Despite their valiant attempts the defending soldiers were doggedly camped behind a hurriedly erected barricade and still held the gate. The grinding of gears and rattle of chain was a clear indication that the gate was being opened.

The Emperor slammed into a small building that had been built against the wall. The door splintered inwards revealing a grain store. The bags stacked to the roof. They had been clearly prepared for all eventualities. Lord Vas took a fleeting look around the edge of the building. Metal spikes struck the corner stones narrowly missing his face.

"We must get to that gate" demanded the Emperor. "If they open it we will be trapped once again." Oma-Sem stood just behind the Emperor.

"I have an idea my Lord, give me some covering fire." Without waiting for a reply Oma-Sem turned and jumped for one of the protruding stones in the great wall. The Emperor and his men opened fire on the barricade. Despite his considerable bulk, Oma-Sem scaled the wall with ease, using the old openings that had once held the wooden scaffolding when it was first built. He hauled himself over the edge and onto the top of the wall. He dived behind a burning grounder just as the return volley of metal shards pinged off the hull. He climbed onto the vehicle and ran, leaping to next. It had stopped burning but was blackened by the assault.

"Does this thing still work?" Oma-Sem barked at the few Reavers lying prone on its roof.   "No idea" one replied.

Oma-Sem snorted his frustration.

"Clear the roof unless you fancy a ride." He flipped open the driver's hatch and lowered himself inside. The controls were stained from smoke but there didn't seem to be too much damage. He pulled the primer lever back hard and pumped the accelerator a few times.

"Come on you nameless heap of bolts" he cursed under his breath as he pressed the ignition button. The engine whined and clicked as the starter tried to engage. It spluttered and then started, but immediately cut out. Oma-Sem thumped his fist into the dashboard.

"Come On!" he shouted. He tried it again, holding his foot on the gas pedal. This time the antiquated engine fired up with a throaty roar. The Dominator didn't waste a second, he pulled the steering lever back and gingerly pressed the accelerator. The grounder teetered on the edge of the wall and then slid over the edge. It smashed through the roof of the grain store and a dust cloud erupted into the street. Despite its weight the grain bags had softened the fall and the battered vehicle turned onto the street, tracks intact. Oma-Sem looked through the small eye slits and aimed the vehicle at the gatehouse. He closed the metal covers and rammed his foot to the floor. The caterpillar tracks squealed at the effort before the grounder took off towards the shocked forces ahead. The vehicle slammed through the makeshift blockade and pounded into the gatehouse. The building was decimated; only the rear of exhausts could be seen sticking out of the carnage.

The Emperor and his men were on the scene in an instant. One defender picked himself off the floor coughing and spitting out the dust in his lungs. He lifted his gaze only to see the downward strike of the Emperor's hammer. Lord Vas placed his foot on the skull of the dead man and pulled back sharply freeing his weapon. He looked around for his next opponent and then chuckled to himself.

His forces were as keen as he was for the taste of battle. The only enemy forces not already fighting for their lives were running back through the town towards the temple. He looked up at the back of the Red Gate. The four mighty bolts holding the gate in place had moved but were still secure. There was no way through for the Virtue's army.

He hefted a wooden beam from the back of the grounder and threw it to the floor. He cleared the debris with his forearm and then climbed into the razed building. He kicked the rear door lever and it popped open. He squeezed his fingers in behind the door and heaved it backwards. The massive muscles in his arms and shoulders strained, but he pulled the door open pushing the rubble away as he did so. He was about to step inside the crew compartment when a smiling face appeared. Oma-Sem was completely covered in white dust apart from a small congealed cut on his forehead.

"Did it work?" He asked. The Emperor smiled and clapped his hand on the Dominator's arm helping him out from the metal tomb.

*

The Emperor's forces defended the wall until early afternoon. They had reached a stalemate as the Virtue's men retreated to a safe distance. Both sides tended to their wounded and shored up their defences. Lord Vas had travelled the length of the line engaging with his men, giving them encouragement and at the same time looking for any weaknesses. He gazed out over the battlements at the massing ranks.

"Looks like they have had their fill for the time being" said the Emperor.

"Yes my Lord." replied Oma-Sem. He paused for a moment and then asked. "What about those cowards who fled into the temple my Lord?"

He had purposely left the few who had escaped for the time being as the defence of the wall was his priority. Now things had settled, he changed focus.

The small band of men moved silently through the narrow cobbled streets. The precarious buildings leaned out over the walkways almost obscuring the light in places. All windows and doors were shut tight only the occasional hound betraying any sign of habitation. The group cleared the houses and reached the start of the twisting staircase that led upwards to the temple entrance. They climbed the smooth steps, worn to a rounded lustre by the thousands of feet that had sought the great temple's sanctuary.

Vas had been here on more than one occasion with his father. The mammoth pillars never failed to impress him. Carved from the rock face, there were no joins unlike the columns that supported his own temple at Ro-Mor. They entered through the exquisitely carved archway which seemed strangely out of centre to the pillars, perhaps some kind of ancient mason's folly.

Inside the temple, the grandeur continued. The main hall which led from the meagre entrance was cavernous. The carved domed roof allowed for the hall to remain unsupported by any further pillars. This uninterrupted space added to its majesty. Huge metal wheels hung from the ceiling way above their heads, slow burning oil giving off a flickering light and multiplying their shadows. Their footsteps echoed as they walked down the main procession route. Either side was filled with a myriad of wooden benches. It was here that those in search of answers or forgiveness sat in contemplation. As they neared the end of the great hall they could see the raised dais. It was surrounded by large candlesticks, and the smell of tallow filled their nostrils. From this point the subterranean building took on a labyrinth persona. Sanctuaries, crypts, prayer rooms and doors led off dozens of corridors at multiple levels. They had met no resistance until now.

Ahead, before a dark statue of a long dead warrior, knelt Fi-Aka. He was flanked by a small retinue of guards and his Principle, Sho-Ota. The two nearest guards stepped to face the oncoming party and lowered their pikes as a sign of their intentions.

Fi-Aka was well aware who had entered his temple and he would play out this situation as he had seen it done before. Even with enemies there was a code of conduct, an unspoken etiquette to which all Dumonii adhered. He knelt for a moment longer, letting the Emperor know he wasn't frightened, at least symbolically. He stood, drew a deep breath and turned to face the newcomers. He clicked his fingers tersely at the two guards; they immediately stood back and withdrew their pikes in relief.

"My Lord..." started Fi-Aka.

"Who is in charge here?" cut in Lord Vas. Fi-Aka looked puzzled by the question.

"I am my Lord" he replied.

"And who might you be?" asked the Emperor. He walked closer to the Virtue tasting the air like a predator stalking its quarry. Fi-Aka gulped. He had seen Vas when he had been a Dominator. He had watched him fight in the ring and knew of his martial skill. Being this close to such a dangerous man was as intimidating as was his muscular frame.

"I am Fi-Aka, the Virtue of Fire" he stammered eventually. The Emperor gazed down at the shaking man, gently stroking his chin.

"I was not aware I had appointed anyone for that position. Tell me Fi .." he paused. "Aka. Did you win this name in combat?" The Virtue tried to reply, but the Emperor continued. "Or perhaps you were gifted this title by those who call me false."

Until this point Fi had believed he could negotiate his way out of the predicament. He saw the malevolent anger boiling in the Emperor's eyes and knew his life was over. The direction from which it came however, he did not expect. From one side Sho-Ota stood forward and plunged a curved dagger into the Virtue's ribcage. The fierce thrust pierced the man's lungs and heart. Sho let go of the hilt and the dead Virtue sagged to the floor. Sho-Ota made his move.

He quickly dropped to one knee.

"I am sorry my Lord" he said confidently. The Emperor had not flinched during the attack; the dead Virtue's guards had been stunned and in that split second the Dominators now held them at sword point. Oma-Sem was at the Emperor's side his sword and gaze focused on the new player. Lord Vas's anger quickly faded and intrigue took its place.

"Can you tell me why you have interrupted me?" he asked as he gestured 'all clear' to Oma-Sem.

"I do not want to offend my Lord. I thought it better to end it quickly rather than have him soil himself." replied Sho-Ota. The Emperor smirked.

"What is your name?"

"Sho-Ota." The smaller man stood to face the Emperor. "I was the Principle to both former Virtues." The Emperor eyed him carefully.

"Tell me, Sho-Ota, why would you kill this man? Do you intend to switch sides? Or were you afraid he might tell me something he shouldn't?" Sho was ready for the question.

"Neither my Lord. Your ascension as Emperor was certainly a shock to most, but I don't believe the people would have opposed you. They are fickle and would follow whoever has the most to offer. The Virtues of this moon have their own agendas, I imagine they wanted the throne for themselves. Whichever of them would have taken it, they would have had no choice but to move against the others. Civil war was inevitable. Fi was just an opportunist. For my part I have followed orders. I now simply want a part in the future. Your future."

"One more thing Sho-Ota" said the Emperor turning on his heel. "I intend to attack the sleeping Virtues at first light tomorrow. I will use the low lying mist to hide my forces. How would you advise me on this plan?" Unknown to the Principle the Emperor had deliberately shown his hand. He believed that sometimes the truth was the best form of interrogation.

"They outnumber your men two to one, you have the superior fighting force, your chances are even. What is certain is that many will die." replied Sho-Ota. The Emperor was satisfied with the Principles accurate assessment.

"There may be another way" added Sho-Ota.

*

The Emperor and the majority of his forces were silently making their way over the wall at the far edge. After long debate the night before, he had finally agreed to allow Oma-Sem to command the remainder of his men and go with Sho-Ota. Vas had wanted to go himself, secretly he wanted to arrive on the field of battle as the triumphant saviour. He knew logically it was better to send one of his Dominators and he remain with the main force. If things went badly, his presence would make the difference.

Sho's plan had been very simple. They had all agreed the longer they stayed at Tetra-Mor the more forces the Virtues would amass. They had not had time to call on troops from their own provinces; the main bulk of the force in the valley was that of the late Virtue of Fire. They had to strike quickly if they stood any chance of victory. Sho had told them of the many tunnels that criss-crossed the interior of the mountain. They were mainly routes of the old lava flow which had been utilised by the Dumonii over time. The end of one such tunnel led beyond the sleeping army of the Virtues. They would travel through the empty shafts and attack from behind at the same time. They had gambled the surprise would give them the advantage and seriously reduce their losses. The Emperor had insisted that Sho-Ota led his men through the maze, if there was any trickery, Oma-Sem would cut his throat.

*

The long line of torches reflected off the low tunnel roof. The column of men had set off in the depths of the night. They had descended a long way down into the bowels of the mountain. Oma-Sem was following the Principle closely trying to remember each turn and twist. After a while he was unsure he could find his way back.

"How much further?" asked the Dominator.

"It's still some way" re-assured Sho-Ota. "We head down again in a short distance; we will be then heading out under the great wall and into the valley."

"Good" grumbled Oma-Sem. "These tunnel walls are beginning to close in on me." The Principle turned, his face partially hidden by the long torch shadows.

"It can take revolutions to get used to it. I must admit I'll be happy to see the morning light." The Dominator looked back along the line of men checking as best he could all was in order. The Principle held up his hand, and the column stopped. He placed his torch in a metal bracket bolted into the rock.

"What now?" asked the Dominator. Sho-Ota pointed to the floor. Set into the floor was a domed metal hatch. The Principle grabbed the wheel that stuck out from the door and turned it. As he rotated the handle, large retaining bolts slowly withdrew from the housing.

"Not the quickest escape route" commented Oma-Sem.

"It's to stop those getting in" answered Sho-Ota. "Give me a hand."

The two men strained to lift the weighty mechanism. As the seal popped, the men closest groaned and held their noses. The big Dominator followed suit.

"Great Shu, what is that smell?" he coughed. The Principle chuckled as he pulled his tunic up over his nose and mouth.

"Sulphur" he replied. "There are still traces of the old volcano down here. It's unpleasant, but harmless." He started to climb down the ladder that had been revealed. It dropped some distance and was illuminated by a red glow. After barking orders to leave a contingent at the hatch the burly Dominator followed into the hole. At the foot of the shaky ladder Oma-Sem gratefully stepped off the last rung and onto the rock. The Cavern they stood in was much wider than anything they had been in before. It was also a great deal higher. Small pools of lava bubbled and plopped throughout the cave. Sho could see the look of concern on the big man's face.

"It's not much further. You can just make out the ledge at the far end. That's it. The door to the valley is just beyond it."

Oma-Sem squinted trying to adjust his vision to the near darkness.

"Okay, let's keep moving." Before they could start into the channel the Principle turned.

"Needless to say, don't touch the orange stuff" he chuckled.

As they made their way carefully along the cave a low gurgle echoed through the underground chamber. Almost in unison the men stopped and held up their torches straining to see where the noise had emanated.

"Anyone see anything?" shouted Oma-Sem. Shouts came back along the line. Whatever it was no-one could see anything. The Dominator turned to question the Principle. To his horror he had vanished.

"Sho" he bellowed.

"This way" came a voice from the distance. The men increased their pace and hurried along the rocky floor trying to catch up with their guide. Sho was waiting at the base of a small rise. As the Dominator neared the low noise echoed once more this time slightly louder.

"What the depths is that?" exclaimed the Dominator.

"It's just the molten rock venting" explained the Principle. "Everything down here is under pressure, as things move air and water escape, that's all. Now help me up to this ledge. The way out is just here."

Oma-Sem crouched down and the smaller man climbed onto his shoulders. The Dominator flexed his leg muscles and lifted his passenger aloft. He walked to the rock face and Sho-Ota used it to stand up on the big man's shoulders. His hands just reached the lip and with a small jump he hauled himself up and over. Oma-Sem waited for a moment and then called out to the Principle. Silence.

"Quick get here" commanded the Dominator. Two men rushed to his aid and knelt to lift him. He caught the top of the ledge and in one fluid movement had crested the rock face. He could see a faint light against the wall ahead. Daylight. He ran towards it and as he did the delicate sign of light faded. He heard the drum and clunk of metal on metal. His gut knotted.

"Sho!" he yelled. His voice echoed out through the vast cavern. Something else answered back. The Dominator composed himself and searched his pockets for his flint. He struck it onto a nearby torch and ripped it off the wall. In front of him was a duplicate of the door they had entered through. He ran to it and grabbed the wheel. He heaved with all his might but he could not budge it. A deafening noise reverberated through the cave. It shook the big man to the core. He ran back to the small ledge. Some had already scaled the short climb the rest were holding up their torches trying to illuminate the sound.

"We have been betrayed" shouted Oma-Sem. The way ahead is locked. We must get back to the ladder..." his voice trailed off as the cause of the noise slowly came into view.

Ahead was a huge beast. It seemed to stop and sniff the air. As it drew nearer one of the men shouted in fear. The monstrous entity quickly turned its head towards the noise and advanced. As it came into sight; the men below scrambled in terrified panic.

The creature was enormous. At least four times the height of a man. It stood on two legs and had long arms that almost touched the floor. Its skin resembled the rock of its surroundings but split between it were what looked like rivulets of lava. As it moved its skin seemed to flow across its body. From what he could see it had no eyes, just a central ridge running over its head and down its back. It threw back its arms and opened its maw. Red light shone from its throat as it once again shook the cave with a deep roar.

"Get yourselves together!" hollered the Dominator. The disciplined soldiers quickly recovered from the initial shock and started to prepare. Bolt guns were drawn and the synchronised hiss of the compressors echoed off the walls. The creature focussed on the sound and placed its humongous arms out in front of it propelling it forward. The helpless soldiers fired at the rampaging beast. Thousands of metal shards found their target, and each one ricocheted harmlessly off the creature's stony skin.

As it approached it lowered its shoulder and rammed into the small cliff. Those on top were thrown backwards, those not quick enough below were pulverised against the rock. Men drew swords and axes and frantically hacked at the monster. Despite their fervour their weapons didn't scratch the creature. In return it flailed madly, crushing anybody that was within reach. Oma-Sem flinched as a fleeing soldier was caught beneath the creature's foot. As it moved again, a bloody pile of flesh and bone was all that was left of the man.

The Dominator dived to the side as a stone fist hammered into the ledge pulping those not quick enough to react. He rolled forward and leapt down to the cave floor. The magma beast let out an ear popping howl. The Dominator snarled his own retort and drew his sword. Before he could launch himself at the monster's torso, its stone hand clubbed him off his feet. He landed hard some distance away. He coughed and winced. His ribs, arms, shoulders and jaw were broken. In a last act of defiance he wanted to shout 'For the Emperor'. But his mouth did not move and he fell silent.

Chapter 5 - Siege

The Titan closed the shutters on the window and brushed the snow from the recessed seat. He turned and watched as his wife Eydis neatly folded the bed sheets and straightened the furs on top. He admired her beauty as much now as he had done when he had first seen her fishing off the pier. How times had changed since those days of innocence.

"I wish you had gone with Agmund and the others" said Lothair idly. Eydis stopped what she was doing and fixed her ice blue eyes on her husband.

"Are you trying to get rid of me now, is that it?" she asked.

"No, no not all, that's not what I meant" stumbled Lothair. "I just wish you were safe, that's all. Whatever happens here it's not going to end well."

"I am sure that you mean you wish I had left so that I would be one less thing to worry about" she countered.

"No. That's not it. I should have stood up to Hagon and moved our people when we had a chance. I have now placed them in danger and the thought of them, and you ...." his voice trailed off.

"As the Titan it is your duty to uphold the law, Hagon gave you little choice. As for me let's not pretend there is anything between us but duty." Her words cut the giant more than any weapon could. She saw the pain in his face.

"Whatever the odds, we are still Magta, you are a great leader." As she returned to her duties she added "You will find a way."

*

His melancholy musings plagued his thoughts as he wound his way down the spiral staircase towards the dungeon. He couldn't shake the face of his brother from his mind. He would do things differently now he told himself. Perhaps there's still time he thought

The damp smell of the holding cells shook him from his memories and he realised that Markus had been talking to him for some time. He followed the Archive Master to the first barred chamber. A young giant stood holding the bars. His eyes were wide and red.

"This is, or rather was, my assistant" explained Markus.

"How much is missing?" asked the Titan ignoring the pleading gaze of the prisoner.

"About fifteen pieces I think. None of the main items I am pleased to say, your maul is still safe. It was mainly smaller items, still all ancient pieces." The old giant glared at Emmerick.

"So what do you know about the visitors camped at our gate?" Lothair now locked the young giant's stare. He saw the clear look of confusion on his face.

"They are here?" asked Emmerick.

"Perhaps you could start by telling us who 'they' might be?" suggested Lothair. Emmerick stepped back from the bars and sat on the edge of the bunk. He regaled his solemn story trying to remember as much as he could about the Mer. He still had enough wit to leave out some of the more self-implicating details.

"So you're telling me that an army of many thousands lays siege to our city because you accidentally killed this man's beast?" The Titan was amazed by his own words.

"An army!" exclaimed Emmerick. "But it was just one man, and a few others that's all, I swear."

"There's more to this than simple revenge" suggested Markus.

"I agree" said Lothair. "Let's go and see what they want."

"What about me" wailed the young giant.

"You best hope they don't ask for your head on a pole."

The Titan making sure he was out of sight of the cowering prisoner turned and smiled at Markus. The Archive Master smiled back.

"That would be too easy" he chuckled.

*

Titan Lothair huffed hot breath into his cupped hands and clapped them together trying to get the circulation flowing. The cold stone of the battlements had chilled his flesh, but not as much as the massing forces that moved out on the sea ice.

For the last three moons thousands of warriors had arrived and set up their tents out on the sea ice. The previously unscarred landscape around the Fortress of Ages had become a constantly crawling stain.

Lothair and the remaining members of the Destructor Caste now stood on top of the fortress walls watching the approaching figure with interest. The newcomer rode a white furred beast. The animal did not seem to be comfortable with its rider and gnashed his head from side to side. The fur clad rider leant forward stroking the head of the brute and seemed to speak to it. The animal quietened and continued its journey towards the gateway. As they neared the wall he hauled up on the reigns and stood up in the stirrups looking up to the giants gathered above.

"He's got grits" whispered Konrad. Before the Titan could reply the small rider bellowed out.

"I am Toll-Son-Ray. I am the leader of the Merthurian people. I would speak with your leader."

"Tie this on" commanded the Titan. Konrad hurried to tie the rope as Lothair climbed out over the battlements. Testing its strength he quickly descended. He stepped through the deep snow to face his adversary. Despite his giant size the rider looked down on him slightly. The beast snorted and saliva dripped from its black mouth. Its lips curled back showing its fangs and its neck muscles bunched as if it was ready to pounce.

The rider again tugged on the reigns trying to restrain the creature.

"My apologies" said Toll-Son-Ray. "I am still trying to break him" He said jovially. "I take it you are the leader of giants."

"I am" replied Lothair." We are Magta, and I am the Titan of this Fortress."

"Indeed" smiled Toll-Son-Ray. "I'll get straight to the point. One of your people took something very precious from me. I have come here to claim my blood oath."

"Is that all?" asked Lothair keeping his voice level. The leader of the Mer tilted his head slightly trying to gauge the emotion of the giant before him.

"That's all." he stated.

"Then why have you brought an army with you?"

"We are nomadic people great Titan, and I must admit I do not like travelling alone." Again he smiled as he stroked the neck of the Shektar trying to placate the fidgeting animal.

"Do not play me for a fool Merthurian" growled the Titan. "Speak plainly or take your steed and go." Toll-Son-Ray's facial expression changed to that of controlled anger.

"The giant that took from me - I want him to face me now."

"So that you can kill him?" asked the Titan.

"No" grinned the rider "So that my Shektar can rend him limb from limb". He patted the animal again and stared intently at the giant.

"And then you and your people will simply leave?" questioned Lothair.

"Of course" replied Toll-Son-Ray. The Titan roared with false laughter. The Shektar reared up at the sound, towering over the giant. The experienced rider held on and quickly regained control, although all signs of patience had vanished from his face, and he made to turn his steed back down the hill.

"Before you go Merthurian" called out Lothair. "We have a custom amongst our people. Instead of engaging in a pitched battle to decide our differences our greatest warriors would fight to death. The winner of the duel decides the terms of surrender. It is a tradition of a more civilised time."

Toll-Son-Ray lent forward in his saddle.

"My champion will meet yours here at first light." He pulled on the reigns and the massive animal turned and loped back down the hill.

*

The structure of the Magta people was that of a caste system. There were four main divisions, Destructor, Protector, Forged and Shining. The origins of the system were lost in history and there was division whether the castes were chosen or dictated. Most now followed in the footsteps of their forebears but there was free choice for those who desired a specific path.

Those in the Protector Caste focused solely on healing. They were the surgeons for body and mind for the ancient race. The vast majority of the population belonged to the Forged Caste. These consisted of the skilled workers, blacksmiths, tanners, wheelwrights and provided the labour backbone for the society. The Shining Caste were the scholars and priests. Their foremost duties revolved around religion, ensuring faith in the old Gods was strong with the masses. The Caste allowed entry to males only. They had performed their remit well as attendance at the Fortress temples was stronger than ever. In these times of hardship the people needed something greater than themselves to believe in. The priests were also the administrators of the Magta. They kept histories, adjudicated on matters of law and kept the mechanics of society in motion, and now as always held the key to power.

The Destructor Caste was once considered the pinnacle of society; it provided the warriors of the giant race. When the Magta had retreated from the world hundreds of seasons ago the need for this Caste diminished. Now barely fifty seasoned warriors remained, most in their senior years. The leader of the Magta people - the Titan now addressed this group.

Lothair had explained the impending duel and the assembled warriors were arguing for the honour to fight. The Titan had put himself forward as the primary candidate.

"Your role is to govern Lothair. No-one here doubts your ability on the field, but should you lose our people will have no leader, it would be chaos." suggested Thorsten.

"Lose?" queried Lothair. Thorsten ignored the comment.

"I am sure that the leader you faced at the gates will not be the one who fights" He continued. "He would send one of his champions, and so must we." The Titan knew the old warrior was right, but the thought of combat had awoken his vigour.

"I will go!" called out Konrad. Although one of the youngest, he was a formidable individual, and tall even for a giant. He had followed in his father's footsteps and joined the Destructor Caste when he had reached manhood. He was aware of the shadow his father cast and had been keen to prove himself worthy. He trained regularly, and his physique clearly showed this effort.

"They are only Dumon after all. Even one of our priests could best them" he added. The equally as muscled older giant sitting next to Konrad now stood. All eyes turned to him.

"My son speaks with the naivety of youth" said the older giant. "Experience has told me never to underestimate an opponent regardless of size, strength or race. One lucky strike is all that it takes, as the Gods are my witness, I know I have had a few." Low chuckles rumbled around the group. "This leader who bravely walks to our gates and demands his terms shows no fear of us. That tells us he is either stupid or he believes he has our measure. He agreed to send one man against our champion. That should tell us something about his commitment. My son is a capable fighter, but I think there is more to this than we know. I will face whatever they send at us." He looked at the gathered warriors and all nodded their approval. They were all aware of his pedigree.

"Egon!" shouted one giant. The chant was repeated and then chorused. The noise from the Destructors echoed around the fortress and carried on the chill wind to the camped army outside. An eye flicked open, the black orb absorbing the fading light. Clawed fingers encircled the metal bars of its cage and the champion of the Merthurian let out an ear-splitting howl.

*

Despite his father's put down the night before Konrad looked on with admiration as the older giant slid his silk shirt over his head. The veteran warrior's torso rippled with sinewy muscle, grey hair covered his wide chest and white scars zigzagged his skin - trophies of past victories. Konrad handed him his padded gambeson and then turned to pick up his father's unique breastplate. The armour was as battered as its owner, dented and scuffed from a lifetime of battle. It was one of the handcrafted pieces that had been previously on display in the Museum and its mangled state betrayed its true power. It was known as the Siren.

The young giant picked up the garment and was amazed at how light it was. He helped his father lace it up ensuring it fitted snugly. Apart from studded vambraces Egon wore no other armour. He argued that the ability to see and hear clearly was more important than wearing a casque, and lack of greaves gave him speed of movement. He hefted his glaive and span it over in his hands relishing the familiar feel of the wood in his grip. Grabbing his tower shield he winked at his son.

"Let's get on with it" grunted the old soldier.

*

Egon stood alone in front of the fortress gates, a statuesque barrier to any that would enter. The entire population lined the fortress walls all desperate for a view of the spectacle. Snow was falling gently, large flakes were steadily covering all signs of life. As the snow delicately landed on Egon's cuirass the armour hummed quietly and the flake vibrated and vanished. The weathered warrior stood silently as he watched the Merthurian circus approach.

A lone warrior led two Shektar that were harnessed to a huge sled. Two massive bone runners supported the wooden housing. The domed top to the sled was covered in animal pelts. The noise of clattering chains sounded as it bumped across the terrain. The animals' muscles strained as they struggled to draw the heavy load up the steep icy slope. Toll-Son-Ray followed behind riding his errant animal and following him were several fur clad soldiers. As they crested the top of the slope Toll-Son-Ray moved ahead and drew his mount in front of the waiting giant.

"So you are the champion of the giants" snorted the rider. "Are you not too old for such an undertaking?" Egon locked eyes with the leader of the Mer and spat onto the ground. Toll-Son-Ray turned in his saddle.

"Unleash the Huron" he shouted. At the sound of his voice two huge clawed hands appeared at the bars of the darkened carriage. The surrounding men were trying to remove the massive metal shackles that held the cage gate in place, all of them clearly nervous of its occupant. The gate swung free and the attending soldiers quickly scattered. Toll-Son-Ray urged his Shektar forward towards the cage. Even this great beast seemed wary of what lurked in the darkness.

"Mighty Huron!" shouted the rider. "We have need of your skills."

"Killllll?" Came the throaty response from within.

"Yes" replied Toll-Son-Ray. In an instant the creature had leapt from the covered sled and bounded over the surprised rider. The Mer leader struggled to calm his ride as the hideous Huron drew itself up to reveal its full height. It flung back its head and howled at the falling snow.

It stood a good arm's length taller than Egon. It looked like some perverse blend of Dumon and Shektar. Standing on two legs, with two colossal arms, it had patchy black fur covering its body. Its face was a mockery of nature. Huge black eyes and long straight fangs, protruding bone and large lumps of flesh which surrounded its head, which was tilted slightly to one side. The disfigured mutation wore only a studded harness and in its razor sharp talons it held a straight length of metal that was serrated along one edge.

The creature eyed the giant and sniffed the air. With amazing speed it soared into the air aiming to bring its cleaver down on its unprepared prey. Egon side stepped and brought his shield up at an angle. The fierce blow sparked off the shield and thundered into the frozen ground. Egon quickly rounded the creature and covering his body with the tall shield thrust his glaive at the creature's exposed midriff. The honed edge sliced into the Huron's flesh. The creature hissed and tried to grab the giant's pole arm. Egon withdrew to a safe distance carefully circling the beast.

As the Huron pulled its blade free from the soil, the seasoned warrior made a second charge, this time holding the glaive at its extremity, he swung it in a wide arc. The creature tried to jump back from the weapon but the length of the pole arm was too great and the blade tip sliced across its shins. The creature landed and roared its defiance at its tormentor.

"You're all spit and wind" came Egon's response.

The creature grabbed its blade with both hands and swung it over head. The metal weapon was blocked by Egon's shield, but he was not able to deflect it. The power of the blow knocked him backwards. The creature pressed its advantage and rained a flurry of blows down onto the shield. The fury of the attack started to weaken the giant's defence. Before he had a chance to recover the Huron ripped the shield away with its claws. The muscles in Egon's shield arm were torn as the broken aegis was snatched and thrown clear. The snarling beast brought the saw blade in a backhand movement slamming against the giant's chest. The sound of the impact echoed across the fortress as the Siren chest plate sang out. Any impact caused the armour to vibrate and resonate. The sound waves shattered the metal cleaver. The Huron staggered back looking down at the broken stave that remained in its paw.

Despite the properties of the cuirass the giant was thrown some distance backwards. He skidded on his back in the snow. The blow had opened a long crack in the Siren. The giant had managed to keep hold of the glaive and he quickly got to his feet spitting blood onto the crisp white canvas.

"Sssspiiitt - Wiiinnnd" growled the creature struggling to form its words.

Egon wasted no time and leapt at the Huron swinging his pole arm above his head. Expecting a slicing action as before it drew it arms up for protection. Egon stopped the spin and thrust out towards the mutant's chest. The beast saw the change but could not stop the metal edge tearing into its torso. It grabbed the haft with one hand and then back-fisted the giant across the face. Egon spun away blood pouring from his shattered nose. He kept his footing and before the Huron could pull the glaive free he moved in again grabbing the wooden shaft and pushing it further home. The creature howled, this time in pain.

It released its grip on the offending weapon and grabbed Egon in its claws. Lifting the struggling giant off the ground the Huron opened its jaws and went to sink its fangs into his shoulder. Those teeth that hit the breastplate shattered instantly. The creature howled again and threw the giant to the floor. The needle-like teeth that had cleared the Siren had ripped clean through Egon's flesh. Even as the creature spat broken teeth on the floor it searched once more for its victim.

Egon rolled on the crimson coloured snow narrowly avoiding the animal's foot as it hammered into the ground. He scrambled through the legs of the man-beast and drew his short curved dagger. Leaping as high as he could he buried the knife in the back of the Huron. Using the hilt to haul himself onto the creature, the blade tore through the shoulder tendons. The beast wailed trying to lift its ruined arm. Egon secured himself behind the creature's head and wrapped his arms around its throat. He jerked his head from side to side as the Huron tried to grab him with its free claw. He held on.

The creature at last found its target and despite the properties of the Siren, the Huron's steel talons dug through the giant's armour and into his flesh. Egon yelled in pain, he grimaced and tightened his grip with his legs and arms. The creature withdrew its arm flinging the shredded back plate out into the distance. In a last desperate attempt to free itself it dug at the arms around its neck. Its strength fading the massive beast fell to its knees. The giant kept his hold and at last the life gave out from the Huron and it fell forward into the snow.

Egon slowly stood blood pouring from his many wounds. Cheers erupted from the battlements behind him and his son appeared at his side offering his assistance. Egon gratefully accepted his son's support as the white furred Shektar of Toll-Son-Ray padded towards them.

"Well fought champion of the giants" said the Merthurian. "Enjoy your victory, for it will be short lived."

"You must uphold the terms of the duel" shouted Konrad.

"It is your ancient ritual not mine." replied Toll-Son-Ray "This has been an appropriate prelude."

"Prelude to what!" shouted the young giant.

"You'll see soon enough." With that he turned his steed and made his way back to the massing army below.

*

Konrad pulled the bowstring back to his pursed lips, his arm trembling slightly with the strain. He looked down the shaft and loosed the arrow. The red fletching spiralled into the distance. The lead rider of the Merthurian was up in his stirrups urging his furred mount forward. The arrow thumped into his chest and the force of the missile threw him backwards despite his own momentum. His Shektar howled at its loss but kept pace towards the fortress walls. The animals and riders rampaging up the hill repeated the cry. The deafening sound washed over the defenders like a snowstorm.

The few other Magta Destructors who had a similar range also unleashed their arrows. The silent shafts all found their targets some skewering men and some beasts. Despite their accuracy the powerful volley made little difference to the thousands of warriors now mounting the crest of the hill.

Titan Lothair looked back over his shoulder to the ranks of archers assembled in the cobbled courts behind the wall. They were mainly the Forged Caste, including women and children. Anyone able had been called to arms. The walls of the fortress were manned by the Destructor and Shining Castes. The warriors had evenly spaced themselves along the battlements interspersed by the priests. Although the remaining Magta had seen little of war or conflict for untold ages, they had quickly galvanised against the impending threat.

The white plumes on Lothair's helm danced as he swivelled his head to and fro. He signalled with his arm and the watching archers released their arrows. The black and red cloud descended on the front ranks of riders. Many fell, shafts sticking out from unprotected flesh. The majority of Shektar continued, their push unaffected by the myriad of barbs penetrating their bodies. Those that fell were trampled by the claws of those behind. The charge did not falter.

The archers sent another volley before the Titan bellowed.

"Fire at will."

Wave after wave of barbed death rained down on the relentless tide of riders. Konrad eyed the oncoming horde keenly picking his targets. Those that looked to command or direct other men became his victims.

"They're not slowing!" he shouted. The speed with which the young giant shot was incredible and had not slowed since his first release. His shoulder muscles were burning with the exertion but each loosed shaft still found its target. He now found himself aiming down at the foot of the wall as the Mer horde reached the walls.

"Archers to the walls!" shouted Lothair. "May the gods grant you all a valiant death." He lifted his gauntleted hand to lower his visor. Now closed, his helm portrayed a fanged skull of an ancient mythical creature. He hoisted his war maul onto his shoulder and leapt to where the first of many ladders clattered against the stonework. He waited as the first attacker crested the top rung before swinging the club. The blow smashed the man's head into a shower of brain and bone and catapulted him back into the shouting mass below. The next warrior was more cautious using a small buckler to try and provide protection. The head of Lothair's maul had started to pulse as the rivulets of blood ran across its surface. The Titan took a deep breath and thundered the hammer downwards.

The maul cracked the shield and skull of the attacker and the power of the blow snapped the rung of the ladder he was standing on. He fell taking those climbing behind with him. Two priests stepped in with long hooked halberds. They placed the blades on the top rung and pushed the ladder backwards. The siege ladder easily fell backwards and thudded into the waiting army below. They were packed so tight that there was no room to move, they could not avoid the falling bodies or equipment that came flying from the ramparts.

The Mer warriors had to dismount in order to climb, so any advantage given to them by their Shektar was lost. They had concentrated their main attack on the colossal wooden gates of the fortress. Two enormous beasts now towed a wheeled ram towards the gate. Konrad was the first to see it and struggled to make his way through his comrades to get a clear view. He notched an arrow and drew back the bowstring. The shaft flew and in a blur punctured the skull of one of the animals hauling the battering ram. The creature's legs buckled under its own weight and the cart veered off to one side as the remaining Shektar still tried to pull the load. As Konrad was about to lose a second shot he saw the first return volley of arrows come sailing over his enemies.

"Take cover!" he shouted as he pinned himself behind a crenellation. Most Destructors had already seen the danger and were swift enough to react. Those that didn't were peppered with white shafts. The archers seemed indiscriminate as their arrows killed defenders and attackers alike.

As Konrad peered over the stonework he could see the soldiers below quickly erecting a roof to the battering ram and moving it by hand into place. Some soldiers braced themselves against the wooden and bone structure, their legs straining to move the siege engine, whilst their comrades held large round shields trying to protect them from the Magta archers.

Konrad turned to look along the wall. All was chaos. The giant champions flung bodies out into the seething army whilst those of the Shining Caste stabbed and slashed at those that escaped the marauding warriors gaze. He saw Lothair's maul plummeting into the chest of a Mer soldier. Blood and bile erupted as the now brightly glowing hammer head tore through the man's body.

"They are focussing on the gate!" yelled Konrad.

The Titan heard the call above the din of battle and nodded towards the young giant. Konrad wasted no time and leapt the few steps from the wall to the top of the gatehouse. Several large metal boxes were stacked at the back.

"Here, help me with these" he shouted at the assembled archers. "Be careful with them" he warned. He grabbed a rope handle and together with a priest they carried the heavy casket to the edge of the gatehouse. Under the battlements were small sloping openings and the two men now manoeuvred the deadly payload into place. Steadying the crate at an angle with one hand and grabbing the metal securing bolt with the other he looked up at the priest.

"Better move back" he suggested. He waited until the other three cases were in place and then nodded. He yanked the bolt hard and the lid popped open. The contents rattled off the stonework and bounced down the slope and out onto the unsuspecting soldiers below. Thousands of tiny grey balls rained down bouncing off the makeshift roof. Hearing the clattering on the roof and seeing the spheres fall, a Merthurian held out his gloved hand to catch one. The small grey ball landed on his palm. Instead of bouncing off, the fatal granule melted through the leather glove and finding bare flesh was rapidly absorbed into his blood stream. A look of horror transfixed his face as the veins in his neck pulsed black. In moments the nightmarish poison found his heart and squeezed the life from it. The dead soldier fell forwards landing on the back of his ally. His own skin now blackened by the disease melted through his own garments and his fellow soldier's furs. He screamed in disgust and tried to push his dead friend away. He looked in disbelief as the veins in his forearm darkened.

The creeping death slowly spread out from the battering ram. Any that came into contact with the hideous virus quickly succumbed to its vile grasp. Panic erupted in the ranks of the Mer as Shektar and soldiers all fell victim to the plague weapon. They quickly withdrew from the source, men trampling each other in desperation to retreat from the invisible enemy. After frantic moments the Mer Army halted. Now with a distance between them and the last of the infected men and beasts they could see its effect. Hundreds of blackened bodies lay fanned out from the central gates of the fortress. A few stragglers from the wall choked and fell dead as they tried to make their way across the carnage.

Lothair, his eyes glowing in unison with his maul, watched as the enemy forces made their way back down the hillside. He placed the hammer against the stone and stood back from the weapon. The red glow slowly faded from the blood soaked head and in turn from his eyes. He had held that section of wall on his own as it was too dangerous for even friends to approach him once the blood-bond had taken hold. The weapon's double edged gift provided its bearer with immense power with every drop of blood that stained its face, giving the Titan unrivalled strength and stamina. Its curse was that the weapon craved all blood and not just that of the wielder's enemies. Over many seasons Lothair had learnt to control the weapon's thirst, but it had been some while since he had felt the euphoria it gave him.

Thorsten approached him cautiously.

"Lothair?" he asked quietly.

"It's alright my friend, I am myself." Thorsten relaxed.

"Shall we burn the bodies?" asked the veteran warrior pointing out towards the mound of corpses surrounding the gate.

"Leave them. It will provide a temporary deterrent against the next attack." Lothair looked at his friend. His eyes still carried a red tinge which made Thorsten wary.

"You think they will come against us again?" he asked surprised.

"We are still breathing, are we not?" came the response.

*

Toll-Son-Ray stepped out from his tent, a light covering of snow fell from the door flap. His Shektar lay nearby and opened a dark eye, lifted its head from its deep sleep and snorted hot breath. The Merthurian leader knelt by the animal's head and stroked it gently.

"Rest my friend" he soothed.

A tall stranger waited at the front of his tent. By the frost on his eyebrows it looked like he had been there for some time. Toll-Son-Ray had ignored him when he had first risen choosing to tend his newly bonded beast instead. He now walked to face the newcomer.

The tall warrior wore the same style of furred clothes as the rest of the sea tribe apart from his gloves and the lower part of his sleeves. They were stained a dark crimson. This striking contrast continued onto the man's face. His face was coloured in the same red ochre, with a black line intersecting each eye. The fearsome looking individual was one of the Merthurian elite legion, the Red Prime.

"Petr my friend" greeted Toll-Son-Ray. "Forgive me, but our bond is still fresh" he indicated towards the sleeping animal.

"I understand" replied Petr.

"What news of the North? Are we ready?" asked the Mer Commander.

"The pack ice is still some distance from our goal. It will be several moons before it is thick enough to cross. We have made camp and are ready when you give the word."

"That suits us well. These old fools inside their castle are proving a stubborn obstacle. How many of the Red Prime have accompanied you?" The soldier shifted his weight for the first time.

"There are around fifty of us, the main force I left in place as you commanded" answered Petr.

"Good. Fifty should be plenty. With your help and the addition of the deep north tribesmen who have just joined us we should take this castle by nightfall" said Toll-Son-Ray rubbing his hands. "I hope you and your men are ready for a fight, these giants are formidable fighters." Petr smiled.

"They have not met the Red Prime" he said confidently.

The forces of the Merthurian continued to swell throughout the morning with the arrival of more fur clad warriors. The last of those to arrive were leading groups of harnessed Shektar pulling enormous sleds. The sea ice creaked under their weight as they rumbled towards the land edge. Making landfall the assembled men started to load ice blocks and rocks into the five open backed sledges.

Toll-Son-Ray was accompanied by Petr both now riding their Shektar. The animals padded up the slope towards the grey fortress. Pulling on the reigns they stopped just short of a black marker flag.

"That's some range" commented the Red Prime captain.

"Yes, although only a few can shoot this distance. We had to remove the insignia from our section commanders as they targeted them first. The rest of the archers have limited range and after yesterday will be running low on arrows" explained Toll-Son-Ray. "The pile of bodies around the gate is where their contact virus started to spread. I have no idea if the area is still contagious, but I will need you and your men to lead a renewed assault on the gate. It will give me time to get our second prong organised." The Red Prime Captain nodded his understanding and with that spurred his mount forwards. The great beast loped across the battlefield at full speed, its rider crouched in the saddle taking the shock in his legs. As the animal neared the field of plagued bodies Petr slipped one leg out from the stirrups and swung down grabbing the nearest limb. The decayed flesh tore easily and he quickly turned the Shektar heading back to Toll-Son-Ray with the lifeless arm in his hands. With his back to the fortress he quickly jerked to one side as a red fletched arrow missed him narrowly. As he neared his leader he slowed and threw the useless appendage to the floor.

"Better to find out now" he smiled as he rode past the impressed Merthurian Leader.

*

As mid afternoon approached, the hordes of Merthurian were once again pouring across the corpse strewn battlefield towards the waiting Magta. This time they did not encounter the waves of arrows as they had before. Single riders fell as they were targeted by the giants' elite archers, but the majority of soldiers made it to the wall unscathed. As they started to assail the defences the casualties once again started to mount.

Petr and his men had quickly reached the gate. Under their fur outer garments they wore thick leather armour and beneath this, floren hide. The skin of the floren had a rubber like constitution and the multiple layers provided efficient armour. They also carried round metal shields each with a spiked central boss. They had left their animals and formed a defensive ring around the battering ram. Stones, pots and assorted missiles bounced off their shield wall as they dragged dead bodies to form a grisly barricade.

A cry rang out from one of the Red Prime and he slumped back against the ram's wheel, a large arrow shaft jutting from his body. The arrow had travelled through his shield, through his body and pinned him to the wooden wheel. Ignoring their fallen comrade the elite guard continued their task. With suitable blockades on either side Petr signalled to the team holding the Shektar. The massive animals pulled on a rope connected to the rear of the battering ram. As it made its distance a warrior yanked a steel pin and the heavy bar crunched into the doors. The metal head of the ram was shaped like the skull of a Shektar etched with runes and prayers and the metal fangs easily splintered the ancient timber. The men of the Red Prime continued about their task with the ram singing out at regular intervals beating a rhythm to the battle.

A soldier scurried back from the front of the battering ram and crouched low behind his shield.

"We're through the gate, but there is only stone behind it. The great ram is making no impact. I think they have sealed themselves in" he reported. Petr looked across the battlefield to where the huge sleds were making their slow progress.

"We need more time. If they believe this gate to be safe then they will focus their attention on the sleds. Scale the wall, we must create a diversion." With his command echoing through the ears of the crouched soldier Petr climbed onto the chassis of the enormous ram. Before he had a chance to scan the gatehouse for the easiest route a giant leapt from the battlements. His weight crashed him through the roof, which he quickly threw to one side covering the reeling soldiers. The nearest soldier jabbed at the giant with his spear, his aim true, but the tip bounced off the giant's greaves and the spear splintered. He attempted to draw his sword but the giant was already on him. The huge figure landed bringing his butterfly axe down with all of his weight. The razor sharp weapon cleaved the shocked man in two spraying blood into the air. As the giant stood his axe blazed out in a wicked arc severing the heads of two more warriors. Petr pulled his right arm back and launched his spear jarring his shoulder with the force of the throw. The giant reacted with amazing speed and deflected the throw with the pronged blade. The spear continued and drove through a struggling soldier's thigh staking him to the floor. The giant swung the mighty axe again cutting through both legs of the trapped soldier. His body somersaulted in the air flicking crimson ichor over the scene.

Petr ran along the top of the ram towards the flailing giant. As he neared, the axe blade swung viciously towards his legs. Petr jumped high into the air and then landed on the giant's outstretched arm before leaping again over his head. As he tumbled forward he lashed out with his short sword. He landed and rolled to one side just in time to avoid the axe as it thudded into the frozen ground. Petr's sword had found its mark and cut deep into the back of the giant's neck. The grave injury did not seem to slow the goliath.

The drilled soldiers of the Red Prime closed on their target stabbing and throwing their spears from all angles. The giant span battering most attacks harmlessly away. A few made it through. One soldier ducked low and came up under the giant's guard, ramming his spear up into the giant's gut. The thrust found soft tissue and the wounded Magta roared in pain. With his free hand he grabbed the crouched man, his massive hand encircling his whole head and then crunched the warrior's face into the battering ram. As he turned, the watchful troopers stabbed again at his exposed back. Bleeding from many wounds the giant twisted again. He wiped the blood from his mouth and exhaled heavily.

He made to step forward but as he did one man dived and drove his sword through the back of the giant's calf. His movement halted the axe swing fell short of its intended victim merely scathing his leather breastplate before slicing through his foot and into the floor. Petr sliced at the giant's hand cutting it deeply. The dying giant reached out for the soldier who had pinned his leg and holding him by his fur coat swung him into Petr. The human club sent him flying, the cold stone of the fortress halting his movement. Petr spluttered as the air in his lungs escaped him. He glanced back to see his men crawling over the still body of the giant repeatedly stabbing the huge carcass. Petr looked out once more across the battlefield and saw that Toll-Son-Ray's plan was working.

The first of the cumbersome sleds made its way slowly towards the wall, hundreds of foot soldiers providing protection for the animals that hauled it. As it neared the bulwark they wheeled sharply and the load teetered before eventually crashing over. The ice and rocks spewed out across the floor. Men quickly ran to unhitch the broken sled, whilst others shifted the debris against the wall. The four remaining sleds emptied their payloads in the same way. The Merthurian army struggled desperately to build the ramp under the constant hail of spears and arrows from the defending giants. Slowly but surely the way into the fortress was taking shape, although it was now layered with dead bodies. Still a man's height from the top Toll-Son-Ray gave the order to his mounted troops. The excited animals bayed as they raced forwards towards the slope. The first rider reached the top and his Shektar lurched upwards its claws raking the stone buttress. As it made to clear the battlements a glowing blur crashed into its skull killing it instantly. Those behind were now urging their mounts to crest the wall. A giant wearing a tall plumed helm raced along the fortification his lustrous red maul falling repeatedly crushing and pulverising any that managed to climb onto the ramparts.

The captain of the Red Prime pulled up close to Toll-Son-Ray.

"The gate is sealed, no way through." he reported.

"It matters not. We will be inside shortly. Although that one giant is proving a difficult obstacle." Toll-Son-Ray gestured to where a defiant figure stood atop the wall denying a foothold to the Mer army. The remaining retinue of Petr's men filed in behind him. The Mer leader looked shocked.

"Where are the rest of your men?" he asked.

The captain's reply was terse.

"Dead."

Without waiting for further orders Petr turned to his men and signalled. The elite guard bounded towards the fray. Petr leant forward in his saddle and whispered to his beast. Hearing the words of its master the hulking animal sped up. Crashing through those riders waiting to file up the ramp the captain made a path towards the defending giant. Using the piled bodies of men and beasts as a springboard the Shektar leapt fangs bared towards its target. The immense animal easily cleared the battlements and collided with the surprised giant. The force of the charge sent the combatants flying backwards. They crashed through the roofs of the houses behind.

The remainder of Petr's men quickly followed and the Red Prime now attacked the giants on their own level. Slowly the mounted cavalry of the Mer flowed into the fortress. Riding their Shektars had now evened the odds against the formidable Magta warriors.

Petr was face down on wooden floorboards. He tried to rise but was covered in debris from the collapsed roof. His Shektar and the giant had broken through the first floor and were in a pile of fur and wood below. His animal was injured, a large sliver of timber sticking through its front leg. Suddenly dust erupted into the air and a huge figure freed himself from the building fragments. The Shektar growled and tried to snap at the giant. Petr watched helpless as the mammoth warrior punched the trapped animal in the side of the head. The deadly blow crushed the beast's skull. Petr wailed. The giant looked up, his eyes glowing red.

"I'll kill you!" hollered Petr.

"Not today" replied the giant. Petr struggled violently to free himself but the weight on his legs was too great. The giant lifted the dead animal and tossed it carelessly to one side. Reaching down to where it had lain he retrieved his still pulsing war hammer.

The rampaging Mer had pushed the giants from the battlements and were now pursuing them through the fortress. As the Red Prime chased their prey through the outer buildings they saw where they were headed.

The Fortress of Ages was built by master masons thousands of seasons ago. They had built the citadel to last for an eternity and to withstand any siege. Ahead of them was another monstrous wall. It enclosed the inner bailey and was at least twice the height of the outer fortifications. Coupled with that a deep gully had been dug from the bedrock along its length. A wooden bridge was all that connected it to the outer buildings. As the riders continued their pursuit the reason for the lack of archers on the main battlements became clear. Thousands of arrows blotted out the remaining light. The chase faltered as hundreds fell under the barrage. As the last giant ran across the drawbridge it started to lift.

Mikel, one of the Red Prime soldiers cursed as he manoeuvred his Shektar under a balcony for cover. To the right of the street a giant came crashing through a building splintering the wooden door that stood in his way. The giant wore a tall plumed helm and had a large maul strapped to his back. He ran full tilt towards the closing bridge. Mikel kicked his heels into his mount and gave chase. Even on his Shektar he was struggling to keep up. The giant reached the lip of the moat and vaulted towards the drawbridge. He clattered into it his right hand grabbing the top. Mikel hauled on the reigns and the claws of the animal dug into the slippery surface stopping just short of the deep chasm. He drew a triple bladed throwing star from his saddle and hurled it at the climbing giant. The spinning weapon chunked into the giant's back. Mikel didn't have time to see whether his throw had achieved his aim as a torrent of arrows hammered into him.

*

Toll-Son-Ray padded towards his waiting men and eyed the inner defences. He chuckled to himself. He shifted his weight in his saddle and looked down at the dusty and bloody soldier beside him.

"Maybe we should have left them to the elements after all Petr?" suggested Toll-Son-Ray

"I am not leaving this place until every last giant lies dead" he spat.

"My sentiments exactly. Although I think it may take a little longer than we expected."

Chapter 6 - Island of Hope

The seablade bounced across the choppy waters on its way back to the Island of Hope. A Medicator struggled to gently dab the Emperor's wounds as the craft rocked to and fro. He had deep cuts on both arms and a stab wound to his lower back. Most of the warriors that had made it to safety bore some injury. Despite the desperate struggle many more made it back to the River of Angels than Vas had dared hope.

The surprise attack had worked well but when Oma-Sem failed to show, the battle became a close fought bloodbath. With both sides suffering heavy losses Lord Vas had ordered a retreat to the fleet of sea craft that waited downstream from Watco-Tun. It was these seablades that now transported the demoralised soldiers back to the capital.

A Dominator approached the Emperor. Congealed blood was matted into his stubble tracing a curved wound along his cheek. A Medicator stepped forward brandishing a clean gauze but the big man waved him away.

"How many?" asked the Emperor without looking up.

"Close to two thousand my Lord" answered Bela-Sem. The Dominator saw the pain in his Emperor's eyes. "I am sure the traitorous Virtues lost three times that" he added. Vas smiled at the Dominator's crude attempt at optimism.

"How many of your brothers fell?" asked Lord Vas.

"Assuming Oma-Sem was betrayed, then just him" replied Bela-Sem.

"As soon as we have returned to the city organise a trial for his replacement. I want you to personally see to it."

"Yes my Lord". The obedient Dominator slapped his forearm across his chest and returned to his duties.

The returning fleet docked at the many floating pontoons. The Virtue of Water was waiting with an assembled entourage. The Emperor hopped from the boat disguising the pain that flared in his back. He walked briskly with Tol-Aka keeping pace.

"How are the food ziggurats fairing?" asked the Emperor.

"It's going well. We have five in full operation and another two that will be ready in a few rotations. It will still be some time until they are producing food, but we have brought in supplies from across the Caucasus Mountains." replied Tol-Aka.

"At least that's some good news. What about the Migration? How many have decided to leave their homes?"

"That's hard to say" started the Virtue "Definitely more than we thought. Civilians from the renegade provinces are also arriving at the island as well as the majority from my own region. They are bringing supplies with them, the only problem will be housing."

"Where are they now?" questioned the Emperor.

"Those who could have filled the communal areas in Sagen-Ita, but most are camped along the coast from Asin-Tun to Devhn-Por" said Tol-Aka.

"And your forces?" continued the Emperor.

"They are stationed all along the coast guarding the food beacons. Why? What did you have in mind?" The Virtue sensed the Emperor planning.

"Leave a security force in place but have the bulk of your men meet me at first light at Asin-Tun. After a night's rest and replenishment we will march towards the town Har-Tun." The Emperor saw the look of concern flash across his friend's face. His father would have never explained himself to anybody, but Vas was nothing like his father. "Don't worry my friend, I am not looking for revenge. I made a mistake on this campaign. I am eager not to make another. Har-Tun is the main grain store of the Virtue of Air. They will not expect any action this soon after Tetra-Mor. It is a good chance to dent their resources."

"You didn't need to explain my Lord" suggested Tol-Aka.

"You are my council, and perhaps my only friend. I value your opinion and you should speak plainly if you do not agree." explained the Emperor.

"My only request is that I be allowed to join you this time." said the Virtue expectantly. The Emperor chuckled.

"Of course!" he laughed, clapping his hand on the smaller man's shoulder.

*

The town of Har-Tun occupied a prominent position on the low slopes of Mount Vitruvius. It was strategically positioned so that it commanded a clear view of the Timocharis Plains and had controlled the flow of goods from the Sea of Vapours to the capital city. The centre of the town was extremely old and was built around the nucleus of an ancient fort. The crooked spires of the fortress still remained and defined its silhouette. Over the revolutions the town had spread out and had swallowed several smaller Habs now sprawled across the hillside.

Events had unfolded quickly since the new Emperor's return and the rebel Virtues had yet to develop a strategy of defence. Instead they were occupied responding to Vas's actions and ensuring he did not get a foothold in their provinces. The general population of the moon were directly governed by the Virtues so generally went along with their laws. Though the Emperor ruled overall his reach had rarely extended beyond the shores of the Sea of Serenity. With the news of civil war disseminating some had chosen to leave home and head towards the Capital, seeking the protection of the Emperor but most had remained, hoping the furore would pass quickly. All Missionrai, Reavers and local militia had been mobilised. The bulk of professional soldiers had been given their marching orders and were assembling at behest of the Virtues. This left many towns and ports poorly defended. Har-Tun, albeit a crucial location, was one such place.

Crude dry stone walls and wooden palisades had been hastily constructed at the main entry points into the town. They were patrolled by a mixture of Reavers and Militia. The town continued to operate as normal and market stalls around the centre were busy with traders.

Shu was high in the sky and it was unusually hot as the Emperor's forces clambered across the rocky scree. They came out above the town unnoticed. The Emperor held the spyglass to his eye, the cold metal a welcome contrast. He scanned the valley and could see the dust cloud created by Tol-Aka and his men as they marched directly towards the town. Focussing his attention on Har-Tun he could see the soldiers frantically running, herding the population and manning the defences. The Emperor was startled as a scraggy looking plaid jumped in front of the hidden men. The plaid were farmed for their meat and roamed freely on the hillside. The harmless creature took no notice of the army secreted amongst the rocks. Following his wayward flock came a skinny shepherd boy. He stopped dead in his tracks as he saw the armed warriors. His mind raced for a decision and unfortunately he chose to run. He made it but a few steps before a circular chakram sliced into his back. The boy flew forwards into the dust. Mot-Sem arrived moments later.

"I am truly sorry" he murmured as his knife sank into the boy's ribcage.

*

Tol-Aka ordered the two grounders to turn side on forming a temporary barricade. The Virtues forces quickly ran in behind the vehicle shield as the two mounted bolt guns opened fire. The compressors wheezed and spat their metal spikes at the crouching soldiers ahead. The volley ripped through the wooden fences like paper. Those foolish enough to use it as cover fell under the barrage. As the splinters and dust descended the defenders returned fire with their hand held bolt guns. The Virtue's men were safely out of range, only the occasional round pinging off the grounder's hull. As the clips emptied the Virtue rose and started to run towards the sentry post. The handful of Reavers were quickly overwhelmed Tol-Aka's lethally sharp sword slicing across one man's face severing his lower jaw. The Virtue's force moved quickly into the town meeting only sporadic resistance. As they neared the spires of the fort, shots rang out. The Virtue's troops took cover under the heavy fire coming from the old castle. They charged doors and ducked behind walls. The town centre had ample cover.

Tor-Ota was alongside the Virtue.

"We are pinned here. Shall I send the Grounders in? They could smash through that wall." he offered.

"No wait Tor. We cannot afford to damage the few grounders we have left. Just keep your eyes on the walls and wait." replied the Virtue. Random gunfire echoed from high walls as the Reavers took pot shots at anything that moved. Loud shouts came from within and the vigilant faces of the defenders disappeared. A black armoured figure could be seen racing along the battlements. He disappeared behind the battlements and then an enemy Reaver came flying out over the parapet thudding into the hard dusty street. The Dominator looked out over his handy work and signalled to the Virtue. Tor-Ota smiled his appreciation and the Virtue led his forces out into the town square. The gates of the fortress tore open and the Emperor strode out his two war hammers folding away in his hands.

"I wish they were all this easy" said the Emperor as he approached. The Dominators barked orders and the soldiers dispersed ransacking the town. They had hitched several trailers behind each grounder and throughout the afternoon piled up supplies stolen from the sacked town. As they neared capacity Mot-Sem came striding up a side street.

"My Lord" he said panting heavily.

"What is it Mot?" asked Lord Vas.

"You have to see this" he said trying poorly to conceal his excitement. The Emperor followed the Dominator down the street and out into the suburbs. This area of the town was home to many warehouses and industrial sites. Mot-Sem entered into a large building, the door hanging on by its top hinge only. Vas entered the building and skidded to a stop, staring at the sight before him. The light streamed in through the high windows. It illuminated a cache of vehicles, mostly grounders, some bigger lorries and the occasional Argos. The warehouse concealed row after row of armoured transport.

"There must be at least thirty!" exclaimed Tol-Aka. Mot-Sem had already climbed on the closest vehicle and dropped into the driver's seat. The gathered men laughed out loud as the throaty growl of the vehicle signalled its healthy status.

*

It had been several rotations since the Emperor's fortunate haul at Har-Tun and he was deep in discussion with the Virtue considering their next course of action. Kay-Ota approached the two men and coughed to signal his presence.

"What is it Kay?" asked the Virtue.

"There is a representative here, apparently from the Virtues. He comes under a banner of truce and requires and audience with the Emperor." explained Kay-Ota. The Emperor raised his eyebrows in genuine surprise.

"Send him in" replied Lord Vas cheerfully. "Do you think he has come to ask for his vehicles back?" joked the Emperor. The smile quickly evaporated from his face as he saw who the Virtues had sent as their emissary. Sho-Ota walked into the chamber. The Principle was flanked by four thick set guards. Vas struggled to quench the fire that burned inside.

"My Lord, this is..."

"I know who he is" interrupted the Emperor. The new arrival looked nervously at his hosts. Vas recovered his composure. "What can we do for you Principle?" asked Lord Vas. Sho thought it was not the best time to tell the Emperor he had taken the role of the Virtue of Fire.

"My Lord" started Sho. "I am here under a flag of truce. I have been given the authority to speak on behalf of the Virtues of..." he paused. "Fire, Air and Earth" he continued. "They wish to put a proposal to you." The Emperor ignored the unknown Virtue's statement.

"What happened to my men?" asked Vas. Sho was shocked by the question; he knew it might arise but he was not prepared for this.

"We were attacked in the lower caverns. A creature from the magma core had us trapped" explained Sho.

"And you were the only one to survive? None of my men have returned?" enquired the Emperor.

"Your Dominator was an incredibly brave man my Lord. He and his men fought the beast and allowed me time to escape. When I returned later there were no survivors." said Sho.

"And you choose to repay their sacrifice by switching sides again? I am amazed you can remember whose side you are on." goaded the Emperor.

"I have done what I can to survive" replied Sho refusing to be baited.

"Of that I have no doubt" said Lord Vas. "What do the false Virtues want?"

Relieved that the Emperor was back on topic he launched into his practised rhetoric.

"The Virtues simply want to avoid further bloodshed. They suggest that the current province boundaries be upheld and that each Virtue rule independently of the throne. They would offer a tribute each revolution in respect of your heritage. Terms to be discussed." stated Sho.

"And what if I do not agree to these terms. What do you think you have in terms of leverage?" probed the Emperor.

"You commented on my plain speaking when we first met my Lord, so I will not trade pleasantries. The forces of the Virtues outnumber you four to one, and whilst your island fortress grants you safety it also cuts you off from the rest of the moon's resources."

"If your army outnumbered my own by, say.. eight to one then maybe you would have a bargaining chip. As we proved at Tetra-Mor strength in numbers counts for nothing." suggested Lord Vas.

"Tetra-Mor also showed that if it becomes a war of attrition then you will lose" retorted Sho. The Emperor paused, contemplating his response carefully.

"Perhaps there is a way forward" said the Emperor. Tol-Aka looked at his friend in disbelief. "Join me in my private chamber and we will talk further" offered Lord Vas. Satisfied that he was winning the war of words Sho followed the imposing figure of the Emperor through onto a balcony overlooking the Sea of Serenity.

"The view is quite stunning from up here" commented Sho casually.

Before he knew what was happening the Emperor had grabbed him and hoisted him above his head. Sho searched for the words to control the situation. All thoughts left his mind as he sailed out over the balcony. The rush of the rocky shore silenced him forever.

The Emperor strolled back into the room.

"After talking with the Principle, he eventually saw the futility in his suggestions and faced with the insurmountable odds decided to take his own life." stated Lord Vas. The gathered guard cast worried glances to each other.

"Tell the Virtues if they want to talk to me, they must come themselves not send an errand boy in their stead" growled Vas. One of the soldiers stepped forward.

"But my Lord, that was one of the Virtues, Sho-Aka was the Virtue of Fire" he explained. The Emperor turned to look back at Tol-Aka.

"How many is that now?" he asked. The Virtue of Water held up three fingers.

"It seems the Virtue of Fire is a dangerous position to hold in these times. There will be no truce or compromise. If the cowardly Virtues of Air and Earth are willing to kneel before me and swear their allegiance then we have something to talk about. You are dismissed."

As the men left Tol-Aka could no longer contain his laughter.

"Took his own life!" he mumbled.

"I can be very persuasive" said Lord Vas.

*

Vas moved the heavy bedspread off his shoulders trying to cool himself down. His head pounded as the fog of alcohol clouded his mind. He tried to remember the events of the previous night but everything was unclear. Cold fingers resting on his arm flexed involuntarily and the movement stung his consciousness like a razor. He now felt the presence and smelt the perfume of the woman lying with him, but any other recollection failed him.

He rubbed his eyes and sat up on the edge of the bed holding his head in his hands trying to squeeze the headache away. The last thing he could remember was agreeing the next course of action with the Virtue of Water and then relaxing in the courtyard with a couple of drinks. How could he feel this bad? As he sat with his head resting in his hands he felt the woman next to him shift her weight and leave the bed. He prepared himself for questions, but none came. He turned to see the slender figure of Danus Venra walking down the corridor her silk night gown caressing her shapely form.

Lord Vas stared at the empty bed expecting it to fill in the blanks in his memory. Whatever happened was lost to him. He looked up once more as the concubine of his father disappeared from view.

*

Danus Venra returned quickly to her chamber. She smashed the small glass vial onto the floor before carefully sweeping the broken glass shards into her scarf and then shaking them out of the window. The drug she had used on the Emperor was a potent mix, she had to be confident that it would suitably disable his memory and render him unconscious. Due to his size she had doubled the dose. Satisfied with her evening's work she dressed and made her way to the central shimmer portal.

The gate was already open the central core swallowing and distorting light as it pulsed in unison with the harmonics coming from the gate keepers. Two guards had been overseeing squads of men and supplies that had been passing through all morning. One looked up and saw Venra approaching.

"Morning my Lady" said the Reaver politely. Venra ignored the soldier and walked directly into the portal. Her essence warped and slid silently into the portal. Instantaneously she appeared in the shimmer gate of Wisdom-Por. The town was mayhem.

After the success of the Emperor's raid on Har-Tun he had pressed his luck and headed for the stronghold of Wisdom-Por on the shores of the Sea of Vapours. His lightning quick attack coupled with the new armour he had acquired had destroyed the defences of the town in an afternoon. His men and equipment were now massing ready for the next push into the heartland of the Virtue of Air and looking to take the temple of Gula-Mor.

Venra moved down the busy streets of the town unnoticed. She made her way into a side alley and through an unmarked door. The shutters to the building were all closed and the only light came from a thick candle on a wooden table.

"Please shut the door" came a voice from the dark. Venra turned and slowly pushed the door closed.

"You are taking a risk coming here in person" she posed.

"Maybe" came the reply. As her eyes adjusted to the darkness she could make out who he was before he had spoken. Over the revolutions Venra had developed an acute sense of smell. She could discern the slightest odours or fragrance and could identify people by this unknown and unique attribute.

"Did you think I would not come?" she asked.

"I have never doubted your resolve my Lady. Your beguiling ways have never ceased to amaze me. Your work with our late Emperor was particularly impressive. It is a great relief to me that I am biologically unaffected by your charm."

"Is that why you came in person? Are you afraid I would seduce your Principles" suggested Venra.

"Absolutely" came the chuckled response. Venra removed a folded piece of parchment from her blouse and slid it across the table. The seated man made to pick it up but Venra's long sharp nail pinned it to the wood.

"Our agreement?" She stated.

"If you keep to your end then I will have no problem in honouring our bargain" replied the man. Venra released her grip on the paper. The hooded man unfolded it and took in its contents.

"Good" said the man. "We will be there at first light, make sure the way is open."

"I will" replied Venra. "You risk much with this venture Alu-Aka, the Emperor will take the temple at Gula-Mor."

"That is the plan my dear" smiled the Virtue of Air. "We have moved all resources from my lands and left a paltry force in residence at the temple. It is unfortunate to lose my seat of power, but with your help that will only be a temporary measure. Regarding your plans I have brought someone to give you a helping hand."

A figure previously unseen and unscented stepped out from the darkness. He was a tall slender man and wore a long hooded cloak similar to that of the Virtue. Venra was genuinely shocked, not as much by his presence but that she had not been able to sense him. She hid her discomfort.

"I do not need a baby sitter. After last night rumours will be rife about the Emperor and I, his guards will think twice before accosting me" she retorted.

"I do not doubt your abilities my lady" placated the Virtue. "However with so much resting on this venture I would be foolish not to provide an insurance plan, just in case you fail."

"As you wish" said Venra sternly "but make sure he doesn't get in my way." The hooded soldier remained still and silent.

"Jak-Te is one of my best men, I trust him with my life and yours" said the Virtue with the slightest hint of menace. Venra kept her ice cold persona in place despite a chill running down her spine as she looked at the tall Missionrai.

"He doesn't say a lot, does he?" asked Venra trying to break the mounting tension.

"That's because he is mute my dear." said the Virtue plainly. He then stood and turned towards the door. Venra understood the meeting was over. "Good luck my lady and may the Gods smile upon us."

"There is just one more thing I wanted to ask you Alu-Aka" started Venra.

"What is it my dear" replied the Virtue.

"Why didn't you get me to just kill Vas last night, it would have been easy" she suggested.

"True" replied Alu-Aka. "A dead Emperor is the end goal, but he must be destroyed in the eyes of his people, they must see his failings. A murdered leader could galvanise those who look in from the edge and worse still they may see him as a martyr. "

Satisfied with the Virtue's logic Venra left the room in a swirl of fabric, closely followed by her newly acquired shadow.

*

Kay-Ota fumbled with the leather straps on the Emperor's armour, the last few were always the most difficult to fasten. The task completed he handed the recently cleaned war hammers to Vas. The Emperor idly flicked the switch on the handle and watched mesmerised as the hammer shaft extended and the head rotated all with a slick oiled action. Kay saw the distant look in the Emperor's eyes and knew immediately what was on his mind.

"I will personally keep an eye on her my Lord" he offered quietly. The Emperor looked at the Principle initially shocked that his thoughts had been so easily read. He chuckled.

"You know my mind better than I do Kay" said Vas. "I have no recollection of what happened last night. I don't even remember speaking to her. She poisoned my father's mind and influenced him to have my mother un-named, perhaps I am next in line for her undivided attention."

"She is a viper my Lord" warned Kay-Ota.

"That she is" said Vas. "Do you know where she is now?"

"I don't but I will find out" assured the Principle.

"She is up to something, I can feel it, and not just in my head" said Vas still trying to rub away the throbbing pain in his skull. "Find her Kay, and place her under house arrest, I'll deal with her when I return from Gula-Mor."

*

Vas strode out from the shimmer portal, light glistening from his white ceramic armour. He now looked every bit the Emperor. Tol-Aka was waiting patiently for him to arrive.

"Apologies for my lateness my friend. It seems as if the Gods decided to pound on my head last night" smiled Vas.

"So I have heard" replied Tol-Aka returning the smile.

"It's not what you think" explained the Emperor.

"Of course not" replied the Virtue quickly returning to current matters. "The troops are in place ready to take the temple. We encountered some renegade groups that provided a few skirmishes but no major problems. I am assuming that the majority of the forces are inside the temple grounds."

"After recent events I would prefer not to assume anything" stated Lord Vas.

The Emperor and his entourage made their way to the main force which had camped in the valley before the temple of Gula-Mor. The circular temple was built on a natural mount that held a commanding position at the confluence of two major rivers. Multi-arched stone bridges spanned the water expanses providing access to the town below the temple. The structure of the great temple reflected its Virtue. Tall slender pillars supported tiered levels that stretched up into the clouds. Some of the higher layers seemed to float as the wispy clouds embraced the building. Unlike most of the other sacred towns on Son-Gebshu, the buildings at the foot of Gula-Mor were unprotected. The two rivers had provided natural protection as had the Herodotus Mountains that loomed in the distance behind. Over its long history the temple of Air had managed to avoid conflict. Its surrounding necklace of fortress towns had kept it safe.

Both rivers were too deep to cross even with the adapted grounders. They were also far too wide for any temporary bridge construction and what boats there were at the port of Wisdom-Por had been scuttled. The nearest crossings were some distance in either direction. The only way in or out was across the bridges. A stout Reaver saluted as the Emperor and Virtue approached.

"Is it mined?" asked Tol-Aka.

"Not that we can see" answered the soldier. "We have been over and under it, I also sent men into the river to look below the water line; we can't find anything" he reported.

"That doesn't make sense" said the Emperor. "The town is unprotected, this is the only route in, only a fool would leave it undefended, and despite his shortcomings the Virtue of Air is no fool."

"What are your orders my Lord?" asked the Reaver. Vas walked towards the bridge and looked out along its length towards the town in the distance. He knew something was wrong but he could not see what. Whatever Alu-Aka's plan he would not leave his temple to be sacked he thought.

"Send the lead grounder across" he ordered. The nervous crew of the armoured carrier manoeuvred the vehicle onto the narrow bridge and made their way slowly across. The tracks of the grounder occasionally scraped the low walls and the driver immediately tried to adjust its path. The Emperor looked on, any moment expecting the rumbling vehicle to explode into a thousand pieces. It reached the other side and lurched to a halt. A relieved looking driver appeared and waved back. The Emperor cast a nervous glance at Tol-Aka. The Virtue shrugged his shoulders.

"I guess there is only one way to find out" he suggested.

"Send the first platoon across" commanded the Emperor. A long line of vehicles and troops now made their way across the bridge. Soldiers looked down over the side each one expecting something to happen. Eventually the last grounder trundled off the stone pier onto the far side.

High up in the temple Leb-Ota gripped the balustrade tightly his anger boiling up inside him.

"What! By all the Gods what is happening?" he yelled. Those gathered had no reply for the seething Principle. "Will somebody tell me why the entire force of the Emperor is strolling across the bridge towards us. Why has the bridge not blown?" Leb-Ota was red in the face, struggling poorly to control his rage and his fear. "We will be butchered!" he continued. He grabbed the shoulder plate of his Missionrai. "Well?" he demanded. The burly Missionrai shrugged off the Principle's hand.

"I do not know. Perhaps the demolition team have been captured?" he suggested vaguely.

"You think!" hollered Leb-Ota.

"I can send another team..." His words were cut off as the Principle slapped him around the face. Both men now filled with anger.

"It's too later for that you idiot" said Leb-Ota through gritted teeth. He turned away from the soldier and stared down once more on the growing troops surrounding the town.

"Get everyone inside the temple, seal the doors and get archers to tiers three and four. We'll not give up the Virtue's seat without a fight." The big Missionrai stalked away barking orders as he descended the spiral staircase.

*

Upstream from the bridge the demolition squad were far from compromised. They were following orders directly from the Virtue of Air and were fully prepared to see them through. They slowly emerged from their hiding place in the rocks above the river. As they made their way down to the water's edge then donned their breathing apparatus and secured the heavy metal weights around their waists.

They submerged beneath the surface and allowed the current to carry them down towards the bridge. The water was murky and visibility was no more than an arm's length. However with the multitude of piers ahead, they were almost certain to find their targets. As the first diver reached the stone column he readied his tether and as the rusted metal eyelet came into view he grabbed for it and clipped himself on. Although the flow of water wasn't that fast the sheer amount of water made it hard to swim against. Now secured at the foot of the bridge pier he felt his way through the silt trying to find the ancient lever.

The bridge had been built at the same time as the temple. The stonemasons had thought of every eventuality and had built in a self destruct mechanism. This secret knowledge had been passed from Virtue to Virtue.

The diver found the handle and pulled back using his legs to lever against the stone. The old machinery groaned protesting at its awakening. Satisfied that events were in motion the diver unclipped himself and swam away downstream. He broke the surface and looked to his side where his comrades also one by one popped to the surface. They looked back as the stone piers crumbled and the antiquated bridge collapsed into the water. The sister bridge which crossed the second river followed its destruction and the flowing waters reclaimed their independence.

The noise of the falling masonry into the water had not gone unnoticed. The Emperor and the Virtue raced to the water's edge. They had been the last to cross.

"That was lucky" commented Tol-Aka. The Emperor looked worried.

"Was it?" he asked.

"We were just on it. Perhaps they have had problems destroying it. We were lucky to get our forces across in time" explained the Virtue.

"Agreed" said Vas. "But we have no way back; it will take revolutions to cross upstream."

"Way back?" questioned Tol-Aka. "We came here to take the temple. It now lies ahead unguarded. There is nothing to stop us."

"Yes my friend. It's like someone wanted us stuck here."

Chapter 7 - The Archaos

Var jumped the small gap from the harbour wall onto Hanelore's ship. He stowed the last of the supplies in the hold. Gero was lashing down a complicated contraption, something Hanelore had been working on. It had been ten moons since their encounter with the kekken. Var was aching to get underway but Hanelore had insisted that they prepared properly for the trip, and that had involved modifications to his ship as well as stocking up on supplies. Var felt a pang of guilt loading the sacks of food when the rest of Asturia was on rations, but sacrifice was the order of the day. He felt that more than most. Bronsur had not spoken to him since he had told her he was leaving to seek an audience with the Magta. He had thought her anger would subside, but he had forgotten how stubborn she could be. He then realised he hadn't made any move to fix the rift either. They would be leaving in moments and he had to speak to her. He leapt back to the pier. Hanelore and Gero saw him run down the harbour. They both knew where he was going so didn't worry about calling after him.

He made it as far as the original harbour before he saw Bronsur running towards him. He hugged her tightly.

"I'm sorry," he whispered.

"Me too" she replied.

"I couldn't leave without saying goodbye" he smiled. Bronsur hung her head.

"I still don't understand why you have to go. We have a good life here. I know things are difficult, but that has never stopped our people before, we have always found a way. We talked about our future here, about children. I am just so scared you won't come back."

"You know the times I sit and stare from the window in our room?" asked Var.

"Yes, of course, I know things have been difficult for you since you lost your leg." replied Bronsur.

"It has nothing to do with my leg. I sit and stare out of the window because I feel like there is something missing from my life."

"What do you mean? Is it something I have done?"

"No, of course not. I have always felt different from everyone else. I always felt like I have another direction in this world, something greater. When I met the kekken for the first time and listened to their prophecy, it felt right, it was the missing piece, my purpose in life. I must see it through to the end."

"What if they are telling you exactly what you want to hear. They read your mind Var! Have you not thought of that!" exclaimed Bronsur.

"Of course I have. Whatever their motives, it still begs the question why? Why me? Why contact us at all? What if they are right? Perhaps there is hope for this planet" replied Var.

"I don't care about the planet Var, I care about us" said Bronsur.

"That's just it. If the weather keeps deteriorating like it has, there will be no us. We had what? A quarter of the season without snow on the ground. The planet is dying Bron, if we..." he paused. "If I don't do something our home, our friends, our city will all disappear under the ice."

"What if there isn't a key? Or even a gate? What if the Gods have already decided our fate?"

"That's all possible" conceded Var. "But I have to try."

"What about Asturia? Do you expect me to keep everything in order just waiting for your return? You are the Doyen of this city. It is you they will look to for guidance" Her anger was unwontedly rising once more.

"The people of the city look to you for guidance. It is you that keeps this city functioning. All I can give them is hope."

"What about me Var? What will you give me?" Tears welled in her eyes.

"I give you my word I will return for you" said Var. Bronsur turned from him and ran from the harbour. Var made his was slowly back to the ship. Gero was standing on the wooden side rail holding on to the rigging. As he saw the dejected figure approach he jumped and landed next to Var.

"It didn't go like that in my head" complained Var.

"I'm convinced women are an entirely different species" said Gero as they climbed aboard.

"You're the last person that should be giving advice on females" interrupted Hanelore.

"Why's that?" asked Var his interest peaked.

"It's a long story" said Gero.

"Well it's at least four moons until we reach Voremerian's Spine" replied Var.

"Maybe" sighed Gero.

Hanelore yelled at Var's two brothers and told them to set about their tasks. The two teenagers shot up into the rigging still pinching and punching each other. Var and Gero untied the mooring ropes and they cast off. Lin was at the helm. She had won the game of 'hands' and so got to skipper the huge Magta craft out from Imercia. The meagre crew hauled on the ropes and wound the hand winches. The heavy canvas sails slowly unfolded and Var ducked as the massive boom swooped over his head. The wind filled the jib and mainsail. The stiff material made a loud snap as it became taught and the ship lurched forward. Var made his way to the bow pulpit and braced himself against the chill wind and sea spray that stung his face. As cold as it was it seemed to cleanse him of his worries and fill him with excitement. Moisture on his eyebrows and eyelashes started to freeze and the skin on his cheeks started to tingle as the freezing wind cooled his blood. He continued to stare into the distance as if battling in some obscure competition. At last he gave in, conceding the win to the elements. He looked down brushing the ice crystals from his eyes. He marvelled at the exquisite craftsmanship of the hurried additions to the boat.

The front of the craft had received the most attention during the refit. The prow of the boat had been coated in a thick metal plate which continued down both sides. It had been installed to provide extra protection when moving through ice-laden seas. There were two additional sails that had been added in front of the jib. Hanelore had called them speed-jibs. They came with their own spars and rigging and were currently neatly tied away. Behind him stood the most impressive piece. Gero had been responsible for this item. He had customised a mounted bolt gun. It was at least twice the size and had four compressors attached to it. The gun part had been replaced by two long tubes and inserted into these were two long metal rods. Each had a screw fixing in the end enabling the attachment of various harpoon tips.

The bit that intrigued Var the most was the construction that now lay covered up on the main deck. Hanelore had been very secretive about it and told him to stay clear of it as it could be dangerous. That translated in Var's mind as 'please examine - this is exciting'.

He knelt down to look under the tarpaulin but instantly found himself being hoisted up by his belt.

"You'll be able to play with that soon enough little Var" laughed Gero uprighting his friend. Var felt embarrassed so tried changing the subject.

"You were going to tell me a story about a woman" probed Var.

"I was" said Gero simply.

"Well go on then" Var insisted.

"When I was a lot younger, probably about your age, I met a truly amazing woman and I fell instantly in love. I kept my feelings hidden from her, but over time we became close and I found out she felt the same way about me."

"So you fell in love, what happened next?" questioned Var.

"Not exactly" answered Gero frowning. "When I say I kept my feelings hidden. I meant just that. I never told her."

"Why not!" exclaimed Var.

"She was promised to another man. A man that I admired. A man who was my friend" Gero said sadly.

"So what. She loved you didn't she. I am sure this so called friend would have understood."

"It wasn't that simple" shrugged the giant.

"Why not?" insisted Var.

"He was my brother" replied Gero. Var was silent. He saw the pain that the memories were restoring. "He was my brother and he was also the Titan."

"What! That idiot Lothair I met seasons ago? He's your brother?" asked Var incredulously.

"Yes. He is."

"So what happened then?" Var knew he was pushing his luck.

"When I refused to tell her how I felt she told Lothair that we were involved anyway. She thought he might release her from her bonds and that we would be together. He didn't. I have never seen him so angry. He declared me Outcaste and well, you know the rest." sighed Gero. Var stared at his friend trying to think of the right words of comfort. Nothing came to him so he slapped the giant on the shoulder.

"Like you said, a different species." Var thought about what Gero had just told him and a thousand more questions flitted into his mind. Gero saw the machinations at work and tried to stem the flow.

"Let's get down below. It will be dark soon and the temperature will drop" He said renewing his gruff tones.

"Just one more question. Does that mean that Hanelore was once the Titan?"

"Yes he was. A great one at that. He stepped aside when Lothair came of age. He said that 'Governance was for the young, as they had the energy to do the right thing but not yet the wisdom to understand why it was right'. He moved away from public life altogether when I was exiled. I think my brother's decision affected him more than me."

"Maybe this mission to find the key will unlock more than we had hoped" suggested Var.

"Don't hold your breath" said Gero. Var inhaled deeply, puffing out his cheeks mocking the giant. Gero swung his fist playfully and Var dived to one side to avoid crashing into the hidden contraption as he rolled. A tall figure appeared from below deck.

"Stay away from that equipment!" shouted Hanelore. "You are worse than your two brothers."

"He started it" said Var pointing sarcastically at his friend.

*

They had travelled for two moons and as they travelled further south the icebergs had increased in size and quantity. Var's two younger brothers Mort and Mido took it in turns to keep look out high up on the main mast. Icicles hung from the rigging and a crisp layer of frost covered most surfaces. The crew had kept to themselves during the journey each lost in their own musings. Lin had begged Var to take her with him. She was still tender from the loss of her father. He knew she needed something to occupy her mind and besides she could handle herself.

Lin was still at the helm. She had listened intently to Hanelore's instruction and enjoyed aligning the strange gimbals that kept them sailing in the right direction. She pulled her scarf up over her nose as the frosty air bit at her skin. Hanelore stood by her shoulder watching her carefully.

"Don't grasp the wheel so hard. Hold it so you can feel the boat's movements. Make small adjustments rather than fight against it" He said. She was about to reply when Mort shouted down from the rigging.

"Ahead!" he hollered. Hanelore fished out the leather bound scope from his pocket and held it up to his eye.

"What is it?" asked Lin. Hanelore was quiet, he brought the scope down and cleaned the lens at both ends with the fur on his coat. He held it up once more tightly closing his other eye.

"Not sure" he said at last. "Looks like some sort of spill around a boat. Perhaps it has lost its cargo. That's strange." He started to climb down from the Helm.

"What's strange?" inquired Lin becoming worried.

"Fetch Gero and Var" he shouted as he slipped along the deck towards the bow.

Var and Gero joined the old giant at the pulpit.

"What is it?" asked Gero. Hanelore turned. He looked paler than usual.

"Drop the mainsail" he said with urgency. Without questioning they quickly set about dropping the colossal sail. As it crumpled upwards the ship slowed. They returned to Hanelore and stared out over the side. They didn't need to ask what was worrying him. Ahead was a huge black slick. At the centre of the spill was a wooden yacht not too dissimilar to the one they were on. Floating on the surface were thousands of objects.

As they neared the anomaly the awful scene became clear. The slick was not created by spilled cargo, but by blood. Dark brown fetid blood. The flotsam consisted of bodies. Thousands of dead kekken, and every associated body part. In between the deathly black detritus were huge bloated white forms. As the bow wave disturbed the peace one such husk turned over. It was clearly a Magta warrior. Var felt bile rise in his throat, and he held his hand over his mouth trying to stifle his natural reaction to such carnage.

The ship made its way through the grisly water and eventually came alongside the ghost ship. Gero threw a rope across and then leapt to the deck of the other ship. The deck was coated in sticky stale blood and bile and he slipped just managing to grab the rail to steady himself.

He looked over the ship. There were claw and weapon marks covering nearly every surface. Discarded blades littered the ship. Gero signalled to his father. Hanelore lofted his great axe across the gap. Re-assured with the familiar haft in his hands Gero crept onto the boat. Before he had a chance to complain Var landed beside him, his two mattocks drawn.

"Hello!" shouted Var. Gero cast him a stern glance. Before Var could argue a noise came from the top cabin. The door had been lacerated but still held. They could hear shuffling and banging coming from behind the door.

"We are friends!" shouted Var, again drawing Gero's chagrin. Var looked down at his feet. His fur boots were now matted in the disgusting substance. Gero's hand shot out holding Var back. The door ahead slowly opened. Out from the cabin emerged a giant.

"Agmund?" asked Gero. The tall giant drew a deep breath. His beard was matted and his face thin. Congealed cuts covered nearly every part of his body. His clothes and armour were torn and ruined. His eyes still shone brightly but it looked as if his mind was some distance away. He lent forward and placed his hands on Gero's shoulders. Agmund stared at him for a brief moment and then buried his head into Gero's furs. Var's friend clearly felt uncomfortable by the encounter. Agmund eventually raised his head.

Page | 152

"I'm sorry Gero, I just can't believe you're real. It's like I have awoken from a nightmare."

"What happened? Where is everyone?" asked Gero. Hanelore appeared alongside the two men.

"Is there anyone else left alive?" he interrupted.

"Yes, four of us; Svan, Baldr and Ingimar. They are not well. They are below." The old giant turned to look back at the shocked faces of Lin and the brothers.

"Lin do you think you can control the ship and follow us out of here. The boys can help. I will come back over when we are clear." Lin nodded her acceptance. Mort and Mido untied the ship and they followed the injured vessel as it made its way through the dire waters and out into the crisp untainted ocean. As the light started to fade, Lin brought the Magta ship alongside once more.

Gero and Var had cleaned the ship as best they could. It still looked like a wave of glass had broken over it, rasping the wood as it withdrew.

Hanelore had attended to the wounds of the other giants and Svan sat mending the sail cloth. His head and both arms were wrapped in bandages. Spots of blood had seeped through in several places betraying the depth of his wounds. Agmund was at the helm, an exhausted look fixed on his face. As Hanelore emerged from the cabin, he beckoned the others to him.

"Baldr is resting, he should recover. I'm not sure about Ingimar, he has a fever. Only time will tell his fate." The old giant turned to Agmund. "This looks very similar to the

Page | 153

encounter Gero and Var had with the Kekken only on a much larger scale." Agmund recognised his cue for an explanation.

"We left the Fortress of ages five moons ago. Lothair had argued the case for leaving the city en masse. However the Shining Caste had other ideas and voted to remain in the city. Food has been scarce for seasons now; the winters have intensified fourfold. Belief in the old Gods is still strong and Hagon managed to persuade enough people to side with him when the vote came to council. The old fools cannot see what is happening right in front of them. Lothair suggested that any who wanted to search for new sources of food should do so. Nearly two hundred of us left on two ships.

"Where is the other ship?" asked Gero.

"I wish I knew" replied Agmund. "Three days ago the skies blackened, some took this as a sign from the Gods in our lack of faith. It didn't rain, but the clouds felt like they were going to press us into the ocean. The heady atmosphere was punctuated by lightning which tore across the sky, threatening at any moment to descend and tear the ships apart. That would have been merciful." Agmund held his head in hands clearly reliving his tormented memories. He drew a deep breath and regained his composure. "The lead vessel was first to be hit. A wave of black creatures swarmed from the oceans like aphids. Moments later they climbed over the rails on our ship. We fought in unison and after an entire morning we had beaten them back. We had lost only a handful of warriors, but of the lead ship there was no sign. They came at us again as darkness fell. That was the longest night of my life. As Shu cast its morning rays I realised there were but a handful of us left. The women and children were all gone. We could see their mutilated bodies floating amongst the Kekken and knew we would be joining them after the next attack. They just wanted to kill. No reason, no motive. Varneer tried to approach them, he placed his sword on the deck as a sign of friendship. They didn't even hesitate and ripped him to pieces. We battled a retreat to the lower deck and barred the door. Even then I thought the door would burst inwards any moment and we would each be eviscerated. I'm not sure what did happen, only that their hideous clicking noises got louder and it sounded like they turned on each other. " The giant sighed deeply. "When it all went quiet, I couldn't bring myself to open the door." His audience remained quiet taking in the loss and horror he had experienced. Gero reached out and grasped Agmund by the forearms.

"You fought like a hero, there is no shame in your actions" he placated.

"It is not my actions that stab at my heart Gero. It is guilt. I am alive and hundreds lie dead. I should have done more." he answered sadly.

"That is not your burden" said Var standing. "I have yet to understand what is happening to our world nor why we face the trials we do. I pray for that clarity but until that happens we must all take the path that calls us. The only crime in these times of change would be inaction. That, Agmund is something you are not guilty of."

"Not all of our kind favour action by the sounds of it" grunted Gero. Ignoring his friend, Var continued.

"We too encountered the Kekken. They had previously made themselves known to me. I quickly realised they had their own agenda but it seemed to mesh with my own. That was until we were attacked. We too would have been overrun, but we were saved by more of the same beasts. They are divided in their thinking, it seems like the hive mind has split. The ones who I communicated with want me to find a key to the gateway to the gods. The others it seems do not. We are headed to the Fortress of Ages to search the archive as we do not know what the key is. I am at a loss as to why they attacked your ships." The tall figure of Agmund stood towering over Var. He clapped his huge hand on the ocean man's shoulder.

"For what it's worth you have my sword." said the giant.

*

The two ships made their way slowly over the calm seas towards Voremerians Spine and the home of the Magta. Var had joined Lin at the helm of Hanelore's ship. He had argued that he could be more helpful there. The truth was the smell of death still lingered aboard the other vessel and he had no stomach for it.

"Why do you think they attacked the giants?" asked Lin.

"I have no idea" replied Var honestly. "Perhaps there is more for us to uncover" he suggested.

"No doubt" said Lin. There was a moment's silence before Lin turned to Var. "You're not what I expected." she said suddenly. Var was surprised by the comment.

"I'm sorry. That is often the reaction I get" he joked.

"No" said Lin quickly. "That's not what I meant. It's just we heard so many stories of the Doyen, how you had united the tribes, defeated the entire Eburus tribe and when I met you, were so..."

"Small?" offered Var. Lin smiled.

"Young is what I was going to say. There is definitely a bigger purpose to your life. I am glad I can be a part of it, even in a small way." She reached a hand out towards his face. Var recoiled immediately feeling uncomfortable and embarrassed by her attentions. The awkward moment was broken by the gruff tones of Gero, shouting from the other boat. Thankful for the excuse Var bounded down the ship to see what the furore was about.

Var didn't think Agmund's face could look any more morose. He was so wrong. As Hanelore relayed the scenes he saw through his scope, it wasn't just Agmund's mood that spiralled downwards.

"Who are they?" asked Var

"I am not sure" replied Hanelore. "I knew there were a few tribes that lived out on the icepack but not in these numbers."

They had made their way to the Voremerians Spine archipelago and were skirting the extremities of the sea ice that extended outwards. In the distance they could make out the rising landfall of the island chain. Hanelore had studied the view for some time. His reports of the massing army surrounding the island and the destruction of part of the fortress had shocked all present. This was supposed to be a safe haven. The Magta were eternal. It seemed as if all history was being re-written.

Under Hanelore's direction the two ships continued South. Hanelore's modified vessel was now leading ploughing the way through the forming ice sheet. Satisfied at the distance between them and the unknown army Hanelore gave the command to drop anchor. He had until now always taken a back seat, allowing Var and Gero to make the decisions simply providing unhelpful advice. The gravity of their situation had seen him change. His air of apathy and cloak of humour had been discarded and Var got a glimpse of the Titan he had once been.

"How long have we got before the ships become trapped in the ice?" asked Var.

"Two moons, maybe three" replied Hanelore.

"It will take at least that to get there and back!" exclaimed Var.

"Let's hope not" said Hanelore. He un-lashed the sheets holding down the contraption on the main deck. The assembled group helped to manhandle the equipment down the wooden ramps and onto the sea ice. Gero attached a metal handle to a gearing mechanism beneath the apparatus. He started to wind. Metal groaned as the gearing pulled and pushed. As the giant continued two large skids unfolded and slowly lifted the platform off the ice. At the same time a tall mast rose into an upright position. As everything clicked into place a sail unfurled sending ice crystals showering over Gero. The big man shook his furs like a animal leaving the water.

Baldr and Ingimar were still too ill to travel and Svan had opted to stay and guard the ships. The rest of the group clambered aboard the ice yacht, taking care to distribute their weight evenly on either side. They had decided to approach the island from the South and scale the cliff. With luck they would avoid the armies camped at the main approach.

The brisk wind filled the sail pushing the sled slowly forward, the two metal skids scraping against the ice. The yacht quickly picked up speed the smooth surface offering little resistance as it skipped across the pack ice. Var pulled his scarf up over his nose and tugged the fur hood down over his head. The sub zero temperatures were amplified by the wind chill as they sped to their destination. The ride although bumpy was exhilarating. The occupants held tightly onto the webbing as they crested a small rise. The sled took off and for a moment the front lifted promising to flip the craft over. Gero and Agmund reacted quickly shifting their bulk forward and sending the yacht thumping back into the ice. The force of the impact sent the sled banking to one side, again the crew now getting a feeling for its movement shifted their weight and brought it back in line. They reeled in the distance quicker than any of them thought possible. As they neared the island the black cliff reared up like a giant tombstone. Var's excitement was quickly replaced with trepidation when he saw the sheer rock face fill his view.

Hanelore pulled a release handle and two metal pronged rakes rotated out from the hull and bounced into the ice chipping chunks as the craft moved. The sail was lowered and Var and Hanelore used their weight to push the spiked brakes into the ice. Eight deep gouges traced their path as they came to a halt.

They departed the craft and eagerly started to push it towards the base of the cliff. They were all too visible against the white backdrop. As they were only a short distance away an arrow sailed over their heads and skittered off the ice behind them. As they looked up they saw six riders mounted on massive white beasts loping towards them. Their riders were all drawing on their bows ready to shoot. Gero moved around to one-side of the craft and bent down placing his gloved hands under the skid. Understanding his actions the others followed suit. Muscles straining they tipped the ice yacht up onto its side. The top of the mast snapped as it toppled over. They crouched behind the makeshift barricade and drew their weapons.

"What the depths are they!" yelled Var as a volley of arrows hammered into the deck of the craft.

"Whatever they are, I don' think they like us" smiled Gero. Within moments the Shektar were on the group, the first massive beast overshooting their position. His clawed feet raked the ice sliding him to a stop. Gero was already in motion. Before the rider had a chance to spur his mount forward the massive twin bladed axe sliced into the creature's neck. Blood spurted upwards covering the rider. Gero reversed his weapon and hammered the spiked haft into the chest of the rider. The powerful blow sent the man skidding backwards onto the ice.

The rest of the Mer scouting party had arrived and were surrounding the group making a more cautious approach. Gero was about to rejoin his friends when he looked down at his feet.

Page | 160

He felt it before he saw it. A colossal black shape beneath the ice. The ice all around started to creak. Air bubbles rushed up from the depths hitting the underside of the pack ice. The animals sensed danger and became skittish their riders struggling to keep them under control. Var looked down at his feet as the piece of ice he was standing on erupted upwards.

The ice cracked and spewed into the air and freezing cold water fountained out from the fissure. The combatants were thrown all ways across the ice, one of the Shektars trying to back pedal as it slipped down a chunk of ice into the waters. From out of the hole came two giant claws smashing into the ice dragging the rest of its body from the freezing sea. A putrid stench assailed the senses as the Archaos opened its gargantuan jaws and roared its hatred at the world.

The creature had spiny segmented armour covering its whole body. Two massive pincers and then a smaller, thinner set next to its mouth. Behind its main claws were six articulated pointed legs that were thumping into the ice trying to give it purchase. Its head was mostly mouth. Its upper jaw extended out over the bottom and two long fangs hung down. On top of its head were dozens of random sized black orbs. Behind its head a spiky carapace stretched out ending in a multitude of sharp bony horns. As the creature turned its head it opened its mouth revealing row upon row of arm length spinal teeth. An oozing black tongue lolled in its maw. The creature was covered in its own microcosm of life. Sponges, corals, shells and smaller crustaceans all clung to its bone armour. Many had been scraped on its rapid exit from the depths.

The Shektar closest to the Archaos was howling trying to back away as the behemoth drove forward. One pincer smashed down into the ice, narrowly missing the mounted rider but with enough force to crack the thick ice. The second claw arced around and closed on the sprawling beast. The rider jumped clear just as the claws closed, cleaving the furred animal in two. The bloody parts of the of the Shektar thudded onto the ice spilling guts and organs. As the two main pincers searched for their next victim the inner claws started to shovel the dead animal into its mouth.

In the chaos Var and his group had been separated. Lin, the two brothers Agmund and Hanelore were running headlong towards the cliff. Var scanned the scene for Gero but he could not see him anywhere. The Archaos once again slammed its immense claws into the ice. The shock waves sent Var tumbling and the ice undulated under the pressure. To one side a floating block bobbed and Var could make out a furred figure in the water. He righted himself and ran towards the struggling giant. He leaped from one piece of ice to another trying to keep his balance on the constantly moving surface.

Gero was tiring. The cold water was biting at his muscles and his mind, his waterlogged clothing was threatening to pull him under. Var landed above him and sprawled himself across the ice reaching out for his friend. His reach was desperately short.

"Hold on!" he yelled frantically. He glimpsed Gero's axe discarded on the ice. He sprung to his feet and scrambled to retrieve the weapon. He lifted the heavy axe with both arms and struggled to drag it back. He knew that he wouldn't be strong enough to hold the weight of Gero. He thumped himself in the side of the head.

"Think!" he yelled to himself. Then, as if the blow had dislodged a thought, he withdrew his razor sharp mattock. He stabbed it downwards through his leg. The unique blade slid through his prosthetic limb and buried itself deep into the ice. He wrapped the leather thong of the axe around his wrist and lent out over the block. Gero was blue, his life force fading fast. He saw Var extend the axe and adrenaline kicked in. He thrust his feet and reached for the lifeline. He grabbed the centre of the weapon just above the butterfly blades and hauled himself out of the water. The weight of the sodden giant pulled on Var's wrist threatening to dislocate his arm. He yelled with pain as Gero tried to climb. The sword anchor started to move in the ice, the pressure pulling it slowly clear. The giant cleared the edge and used Var's body to pull himself all the way up. Var's arm felt limp as he tried to raise the weapon.

Exhausted the two friends lay panting, the freezing air now burning their tired lungs. There was no time to rest as the ice block bobbed violently under another blow from the Archaos. Gero tore off his saturated fur coat and threw it into the water. He helped Var with his axe and then crouched next to him.

"Thank you" he said with every ounce of sincerity he could muster.

"We're even now" smiled Var.

The two men quickly vaulted their way back to the pack ice. They looked over their shoulders to see the titanic creature scoop the last remnants of a Mer warrior into its mouth. The creature tilted its head and the two men appeared in its multi faceted eyes.

"Get to the rock!" shouted Gero. They ran. Gero's huge stride got him there first. Var although accomplished on his artificial leg was struggling. Stabbing his sword through the leg had damaged some of the springs and the leg was now slowing him down. The Archaos was heading directly for them its thirst for flesh not even slightly sated.

The rest of the group had started to make their way up the cliff. Lin had initially thought they would have to climb. But Hanelore showed them a series of chipped ledges that led zigzagging up the rock face. They looked to the untrained eye like natural features, but had been hand carved by the Magta. Lin and the brothers found the ascent easy. The hidden path had been made for giant feet.

Gero started the climb looking back for Var.

"Go!" shouted Var awkwardly running and half hopping towards him. Gero remained where he was until Var reached him. He grabbed Var and swung him onto his back and began to climb along the ledge. The Archaos was steadily thumping its way towards them. As it saw its prey climb its actions became faster and it scrabbled towards the cliff. The rest of the group had stopped way up the cliff safe from the reach of the creature. Agmund started downwards. Gero climbed as fast as his numb fingers would allow working at first one way and then the other climbing upwards all the while. He looked back. The Archaos bellowed as it reached the cliff. The giant looked up and saw Agmund reaching out. He grabbed Var and holding him by the belt unceremoniously threw him upwards. Agmund caught him and dragged him to the narrow path. Gero span to see the vast claw coming fast towards him. He jumped and grabbed Agmund's outstretched hand. The second giant dragged him upwards just as the spiny claw pounded into the rock. Fragments exploded in all directions and large sections of the cliff face tumbled towards the ice. The agitated Archaos was clawing against the rock repeatedly swinging its pincers into the rock trying to dislodge its quarry.

Suddenly it stopped. It swung its carapace around and raised its head as if sniffing the air. Out across the ice plains the ruckus had attracted the attention of the Mer army. A mounted squad was now making its way towards them. The creature sensed the oncoming meal and disappeared back through the crater it had emerged from.

The two giants and Var sat on the precarious ledge staring blankly at the swirling water where the creature had just submerged.

"That was interesting" breathed Var.

"No my friend, that was close" chuckled Gero. Laughter rang out across the icy plains. The sound faded and was replaced by the cracking of ice as a sinister dark shape moved under the feet of the advancing Mer.

Chapter 8 - Abandon Hope

The shimmer portals had been around for as long as memory served. They had been the reason the forefathers had been able to leave the drowning planet and escape to the relative safety of its moon. Although the intricacy of how they worked was lost wisdom, they retained enough knowledge to operate them successfully. Most towns had access to a gateway. Some were small that allowed only a single person through at a time. Others were much larger allowing vehicles and large groups to travel together. A few gates were also amplified and allowed travel over vast distances. These gates were used to jump to the surface of the ocean planet Gebshu. Since his return Lord Vas had destroyed all but one in his attempt to sever all ties with their long forgotten home world.

The gate system required only that one end was opened. The Harmonic chants would open the portal, and the subtle tones would determine the connecting location. Travel could only be made from one gate to another, as any other form risked that the destination was occupied by something else. That meant a gruesome death or worse still a hideous melded deformity.

Since the start of the civil war travel through the gates had been restricted. The Emperor wanted to destroy all of the gates within his domain but he had been advised against it. They had dismantled a few but those that survived now retained a permanent guard and a team of servitors who shared shifts at the gate, chanting a rhythm of closure. As long as the guttural mumblings of the gatekeepers remained, travel to that particular gate was not possible.

All of the shimmer portals on the Island of Hope were sealed. The only way onto the island was by boat. The port of Asin-Tun was now the main transport hub for the forces of the Emperor. It was through this portal that Danus Venra and Jak-Te casually strolled.

The odd couple made their way out along one of the myriad of floating pontoons that stretched out into the sea. Each had cargo and personnel vessels docked alongside. It was the busiest it had been in revolutions. As the two passengers approached a small dhow, a misshapen character bumbled towards them.

"Mistress! Mistress!" he warbled.

"What is it Pol" asked Venra concerned.

"Quickly come on board, I have urgent news." Venra and the Missionrai followed the small man onto the boat. Pol-I was almost unique in his stature amongst the Dumonii. He had been born with growth defects. It had stunted his height giving him unusually short legs and arms. His lot did not end there. Whatever had caused his height deformity had also disfigured his face. One side looked inflated and the skin above his eye folded down obscuring his vision.

The Dumonii society did not tolerate weakness, and physical or mental corruption were usually dealt with as soon as they became noticeable. For that reason it was unusual to see someone of Pol-I's appearance reach adulthood. He owed his existence entirely to Danus Venra and her family. She had been a child when she had first met him. Her parents had used their significant influence to help him avoid the cut. As they grew up

Venra quickly saw an ally in her strange looking friend. No matter what she had asked him to do, he did it without question. She had used her sharp tongue and womanly guile to stop the verbal and physical abuse he received and soon he became an associated and moderately accepted part of his beautiful saviour.

"You cannot return to the island mistress" said Pol-I urgently.

"Why not, what has happened?" enquired Venra.

"The Emperor does not trust you. I don't know what you did to him but he did not like it. He has ordered your arrest on return to the palace." In a second the watching figure of Jak-Te flashed into action drawing a curved dagger and twirling the shocked woman around. He held her with one arm around the neck and the other held the keen edge against her throat. Pol-I jumped up drawing his own blade.

"Wait!" yelled Venra. She signalled to her servant to hold. "The plan is still sound" she pleaded. "I do not need to return to the island, we can still bring the Virtue's men to Devhn-Por as planned. It just means the task will be more difficult. I am sure you are up for the challenge?"

Jak-Te meticulously withdrew his knife slowly releasing his captive. He nodded, and then indicated they should go.

"It's Okay Pol" soothed Venra. "I am fine. Take us down the coast to Devhn-Por." She stroked his shoulder and then kissed him gently on the forehead. The small man disappeared to ready the dhow. Venra noticed the look of disgust on the Missionrai's face.

"Do not underestimate the conviction of love" she chided. The tall warrior ignored her and ducked to leave the cabin. Venra seethed with fury. She was not used to this lack of control over men. Alu-Aka knew what he was doing sending a mute soldier. She could not enter into a conversation with him and twist his words, but perhaps he would react to her other talents.

*

It was late afternoon as Pol-I collapsed the sail and they moored the boat on a small deserted beach. They had decided against landing at the port just in case the Emperor's orders had stretched that far. Securing the shimmer portal at Devhn-Por would be more complicated without the help of her household. Watching the tall soldier leap from the boat brought the price of failure to the forefront of her thoughts.

"Take the boat back to the island Pol, and wait for me there" Venra explained.

"But mistress" complained Pol-I.

"You know the plan, I will need you there, I cannot risk suspicion." It was hard to distinguish emotions on his distorted face, but Venra clearly saw the look of sadness.

"It is the right thing to do, you know that don't you Pol" she soothed. Pol-I nodded and set about preparing the boat.

Venra and Jak-Te set off along the coast path towards the town. As they reached the cliff top they looked down across the open plains. The brilliant light from the food beacons made them squint and cover their eyes. The ziggurats stood like ethereal vanguards watching over the people of the river delta. Blinded by the dazzling sight Venra did not see the small group of men marching towards them. As they formed from the light she realised it was too late to run or hide. She looked over her shoulder to instruct the Missionrai to follow her lead. He was already gone.

Venra walked directly at the five soldiers, ensuring her hips were swaying suitably.

"Good afternoon gentleman" she said tilting her head in a sign of respect. The lead soldier turned to his squad.

"I'll handle this lads" he whispered, and then turned to face Venra.

"Good afternoon my lady. May I ask what you are doing this far out from town" he asked vaguely trying to hide his lust.

"Is it a crime to go walking?" asked Venra ignoring the man's clear disregard for her status.

"Well actually, yes it is. Unless you have been authorised to be out here or are part of the pyramid teams then it is an offence." explained the man licking his lips.

"Do you know who I am?" she asked.

"I am afraid you have me at a loss ma'am" said the soldier putting on the most aristocratic voice he could muster.

"I am Danus Venra." The man looked genuinely shocked. They had all heard of her. He turned and huddled together with the others. Laughter emanated from the group and the guard turned.

"My apologies Danus Venra. We are only lowly soldiers and were not advised of your arrival."

"That's not a problem" replied Venra. "I will be on my way into town." She nodded once more and made to move past the lead man. He stood to block her way.

"You still need to show me your pass, or maybe.." his voice trailed off and he rubbed his chin. "Maybe a kiss would allow me to let you pass." Venra eyed the foul smelling man carefully.

"A simple kiss, is that all?" she asked politely.

"Aye, that's all... for me. My mates though, I'm not sure they will be so easily pleased." The group of men laughed their fervour rising. The carnal gleam in the guard's eye was quickly extinguished as Venra jabbed her long hair pin into his eye popping the organ. The shocked man stumbled back into his friends screaming and holding his face. Ignoring the stricken guard the men drew their weapons and advanced.

Venra casually unwound the belt around her tunic and it voluntarily unfurled. Holding one end she lifted her arm up and then thrust it down quickly. The belt separated into three strands, and the metal ends cracked in unison as she expertly wielded the whip. She swung her arms casting the weapon towards the oncoming posse. The razor sharp ends lashed across one man's face cutting deeply into his flesh. She repeated the action as another soldier tried to dash forward. The whip cut cleanly through his breastplate and opened a massive wound in his stomach. The two remaining men were now more apprehensive but still determined.

The taller of the two men launched a throwing axe and then followed it in drawing his sword. Venra ducked beneath the spinning weapon and lashed out once more with the venomous whip. This time the low strike caught the rushing soldier square in the groin. The sharp barbs tearing through fabric and flesh. As she recovered her balance she struck at the last warrior. He held his arm up to shield his body. The whip wrapped around his arm cutting into his bicep. He grimaced at the pain but held onto the whip as Venra tried to jerk it free.

"Got you now whore" he goaded. Before Venra had a chance to act a glistening throwing star chunked into the side of the man's head. He dropped dead. Jak-Te emerged from the bushes smiling.

"You took your time" she scowled. The tall Missionrai just shrugged his shoulders and proceeded to silence the fallen soldiers.

After securing the bodies in the undergrowth the remaining trip into town was uneventful. Despite the place being overrun with soldiers, they were preoccupied with their own duties most of which centred around supply of the food pyramids. The first to be planted would soon be ready for harvesting. The shimmer portal was inside the municipal hall. The building was unusually grand for the size of the town, six large columns supported a triangular frontage on three sides. Each had statues decorating the apex of each entrance. The main square roof was punctuated by a circular tower which had a ornate domed roof. Venra and the Missionrai checked into a small tavern facing their target.

Jak-Te stretched out on one of the small beds and fell instantly to sleep. Venra sat looking out of the window. She knew she wouldn't get much sleep. Pangs of doubt crept into her mind as the town square thronged with people, mostly soldiers. There would be more inside the building and without help it would take a miracle to secure the gate. Just then that miracle walked across the square towards the hall.

He was a rotund man, balding and sweating from the exertion of walking. He had a large gold chain around his neck indicating a seal of office of some kind. Venra's mind immediately sprang to life and she quietly opened the door and bounded down the stairs. She quickly caught up with the man and started to exude her womanly charm.

*

Jak-Te awoke to see Venra sat staring from the window of the tavern.

"Good, you're awake" she said. "We need to go soon I am just waiting for... There. That's the signal, let's go. If you could make yourself invisible again until we are inside the building I would be grateful."

Venra crept across the square and to one side of the town hall. She walked up to a side door and put her ear to it. She could hear heavy footsteps inside. The lock creaked and the door opened to reveal a large red faced man.

"They have all gone" he whispered. "Only the gate guards are left. We have the place to ourselves." Saliva dripped from one side of his mouth in expectation. Venra stroked his cheek and led him inside. As he turned to lock the door she
Page | 173

drew her hairpin and thrust it into his neck. He coughed and spluttered as he stumbled in the hallway. Jak-Te appeared in the door frame and quickly jumped onto the stricken man covering his mouth to silence his cries. He looked up at Venra with an angry snarl. Ignoring him she stepped over the body and locked the door.

The noise had attracted one of the guards who was walking leisurely down the corridor to investigate. He saw the body of the councillor and the two intruders and drew his sword. Jak-Te followed suit. His sword was as long as his arm, thin and had a subtle curve. Most of the Dumonii swords were thick, heavy weapons designed to hack, slash and bludgeon their opponents. Jak-Te's sword required speed, finesse and accuracy, traits he had in abundance.

Despite the narrow corridor the guard swung widely. Jak-Te ducked beneath the swing as it crashed into the brickwork. He thrust out his sword and the keen edge sliced along the man's bicep. The weighty weapon dropped from his hand as Jak-Te swivelled driving his blade up under the helpless guard's ribcage and through his heart. He withdrew it as swiftly as it had entered. He grabbed the dead man's collar and gently lowered him to the flagstones.

The two assassins made their way through the corridors and out into the main chamber. The low grumble of the servitor could be heard, and occasional laughter coming from a balcony above. Jak-Te signalled upwards. He then pointed at Venra and signalled towards the crossed legged servitor at the centre of the gate. Venra nodded.

Removing her shoes she crept towards her innocent victim. She pulled one of the long spikes holding her hair in place and positioning herself directly behind him, jabbed the poison tipped hair pin into his neck. His prayers of closure ceased and he slumped to the floor. Even though the low noise he had been making seemed to merge with the background the guards above instantly noticed its loss. One looked over the balcony.

"Intruders!!" he bellowed. He reached down by his side and hefted a large crossbow. The weapon was already cocked and he quickly placed a bolt into the channel. Venra was running for cover and Jak-Te was running towards the four guards. The guard let fly with the crossbow. The bolt hammered into Venra's shoulder sending her sprawling across the polished floor. As the guard turned, a throwing star sliced into his forehead. The three remaining guards leapt to their feet spilling the table and its contents. Before they knew what was happening the nearest soldier was holding his neck, blood spurting out across the others from a deep cut in his throat. His desperate efforts to stem the flow were futile and his lifeblood continued to pump out from between his fingers. Wiping his friend's blood from his eyes the nearest Reaver managed to grab the hilt of his sword. He didn't have time to draw the weapon as Jak-Te's blade tore through his stomach. The last soldier had already decided on his course of action and was running headlong towards the circular window at the end of the mezzanine. Jak-Te unbuckled another throwing star and with an overhead throw launched it after the fleeing guard. It caught him square in the back, the long spikes puncturing through his armour. It had wounded him but not stopped him. The flailing guard threw his sword away and dived towards the window. His weight smashed through the glass and timber frame and he fell with a thud into the dusty town square below. Jak-Te held onto the ruined window frame and peered out. Despite the fall, the soldier was still moving and trying to pick himself up.

The Missionrai retrieved the dead guard's crossbow and with his foot in the stirrup pulled back the bow string. Securely hitched he loaded a bolt. As he returned to the broken window the man had found his feet and was tottering away. He made it only a few steps before the metal bolt shattered his skull.

As Jak-Te made his way down the stairs he saw Venra attempting to slide a heavy table in front of the main doors. The bolt was still protruding from her back.

"Quickly! We must block the doors, or we'll be dead before first light" she cried with an unusual sense of urgency. They continued to block the entrances to the hall with everything available. It was just past midnight and would be some time before the Virtue's army would arrive through the portal. They made their way back to the mezzanine and looked out from the window. They could still make out the dead body in the darkness and luckily the rest of the town square was as still.

Jak-Te made to look at the crossbow bolt embedded in Venra's shoulder. She pulled away.

"Don't touch me" she hissed. Unaffected by her protests the Missionrai carefully tore her dress to inspect the wound. The bolt was buried deep and he suspected it had pierced the scapula. He could do more damage if he attempted to remove it. Venra looked at him clearly in pain.

"Can you remove it?" she asked. He shook his head.

"Let's hope the Alu-Aka is early" said Venra quietly.

The night dragged, each passing moment seeming to last forever. The occasional person could be heard in the distant streets but luckily none came close the main hall. A dull glimmer stealthily crept its way over the rooftops signalling the start of the day. With it came more people and it wasn't long before the body was found and the alarm raised. Soldiers came pouring out from the hostels and taverns, some still buttoning gambesons and lacing boots.

As the first soldier approached the doors, Jak-Te loosed a well aimed bolt. It struck the man in the side of the face smashing his teeth as it tore through his cheek. In temporary panic the growing retinue withdrew. It wasn't long before courage returned and this time a shielded squad made its way towards the town hall entrance. The soldiers kicked and shoulder charged the door with little effect. Orders were passed back and four men carrying a heavy metal post joined the group. The thumping repetition rang out in the early morning, like temple bells announcing the break of the day. Slowly the steady hammering started to splinter the door.

Inside Venra and Jak-Te were behind the blockade desperately trying to think of ways to slow the soldiers on the outside. The lithe Missionrai clambered on top of the debris behind the door and drew his sword. As light pierced the timber he thrust his sword through the gap. He felt the weight of flesh at the other end and withdrew the blood soaked blade. He repeated the process at every opportunity. It reminded Venra of a children's circus game where they had to hit the wooden pegs as they appeared from holes, only with blood and a far more serious outcome.

The soldiers at the gate had started to mirror Jak-Te's tactic, thrusting spears and swords through the gaps trying to skewer their tormentor. Several attempts came close and the Missionrai was bleeding from several cuts on his legs and arms. As the door slowly gave way Jak-Te's movements became more desperate. He sliced, jabbed and jumped across the blockade trying to keep the soldiers at bay. Although she intensely disliked the man, she could not help but admire his dedication and his considerable skill. She thought to help him but any movement now sent shivers of pain through her body. The loss of blood was taking its toll.

Jak-Te deflected a spear, slicing through the wooden haft, but a second pike rammed into his calf. If he could have cried in pain, he would have. He swung his sword downwards and the mottled patina of his blade cut cleanly through the weapon's shaft. He looked down at his ruined leg just as a sword blade came bursting through the door. The wide blade cleaved a hole in his breastplate and impaled him. As the soldier on the other side drew back his sword he pulled the stricken Missionrai into the door, his face colliding with the splintered timber.

Against all the odds Jak-Te placed his hands against the door and pushed himself backwards, freeing himself from the blade. He rolled back on the tables and chairs that were barring the entrance dark blood oozing from the wound in his chest. With his life force ebbing he drew a flint from his pocket and feebly tried to strike it. Venra watched transfixed as the metal flint fell from Jak-Te's dead hand and clattered onto the marble floor.

She closed her eyes as the door shattered inwards. Behind her at the centre of the shimmer portal the light started to fold as if viewed through a poorly crafted glass pane. In an instant a hum of energy filled the room and soldiers materialised at the core of the gate. They poured through, in unified ranks like an unstoppable flow of magma. The crude barricade and the lifeless body of Jak-Te were cast aside as the Virtue of Air's men sought combat.

Her vision blurring she saw the unmistakably camp posture of Alu-Aka loom over her.

"Well done my dear" said the Virtue. "May I enquire what happened to my emissary?" Venra pointed towards the discarded figure by the entrance.

"Oh, I see" said the Virtue nonplussed. "That looks like a nasty injury, hopefully it will be enough to convince the Emperor of your innocence. We should talk about your next mission."

"What next mission? This was it. This was the deal!" exclaimed Venra coughing with pain.

"The deal has changed. You have proven your worth. So much so that you are a victim of your own success my dear. If you can open the way here perhaps you can do the same for me on the Island of Hope."

Venra didn't reply.

*

It was two rotations hard march before the Emperor and his men returned to the port of Wisdom-Por. They had sacked the temple of Gula-Mor but it was a hollow victory. The defenders had fought with purpose and Vas had lost more men than he expected storming the towering bastion. Once secure the futility of the venture had hit him like a battering ram. He had been buoyed by his previous successes and that had motivated him to take the Virtue of Air's seat of power. As he marched his men towards the shimmering portal he realised he had been galvanised by revenge and hatred rather than a strategic motive. His men didn't see it that way. They were jubilant off the back of a third victory and following an invincible leader.

The Servitor in charge of opening the portal came before the Emperor. He saluted meekly.

"My Lord, forgive me, but there is a problem with the gate."

"What is it?" asked Lord Vas.

"I cannot establish a link with our gate at Asin-Tun. It is like there is a closure chant upon it."

"What about Angel-Por?" questioned the concerned Emperor.

"I have already tried that. It too is closed, the only gate open to us is at Devhn-Por."

"Something's wrong" growled Vas. The Virtue of Water approached to see what the holdup was about.

"Problems?" he asked cheerfully.

"All of the gates are closed to us except Devhn-Por. I have a really bad feeling about this."

"Why can't we travel there. You can see the progress we have made on the food beacons." suggested Tol-Aka.

"No. It feels wrong. Where is Kay? Ask him to attend immediately." Tol-Aka had just been speaking with the Principle so made his way back to find him. The Emperor turned to the waiting Servitor. "Prepare to open a link back to the Island of Hope. You will only have a small window."

"Yes my Lord" replied the Servitor not understanding what was happening.

Kay-Ota and the Virtue returned and the Emperor explained the situation and his idea. Although all of the gates on the Island of Hope were sealed, and travel to the island had been by boat only, the Emperor had organised an emergency procedure.

"I hope this works" said Lord Vas. "Otherwise it's a long trek back to the coast." They waited patiently as the squad that Kay-Ota had instructed made their way out from the town. It was an uncomfortable wait and eventually Tol-Aka shouted out.

"There!"

Some way from the town and now rising sharply into the sky was a red glowing orb. A thin smoke trail wisped behind it as it finally reached its apex high above. It started to fall but then exploded. The crack echoed off the valley walls and streamers of red light cascaded out from the detonation point.

"I hope they see it" said Tol-Aka.

"If they didn't see it, I'm sure they heard it" replied Kay-Ota.

The Servitors at the gate waved frantically towards the Emperor.

"It's open, let's go" commanded Lord Vas.

*

Vas sat slumped in his throne. His spirit struggling for consciousness. Bela-Sem led a prisoner towards him. Her hands were bound behind her back and the big Dominator had her hold tightly around the upper arm. Her hair was matted and hung down around her dirt and blood encrusted face. Her right eye was a deep purple and completely closed. A crude bandage around her shoulder oozed blood. Her glamour and posture had deserted her completely. Vas sighed and a pang of pity struck him as he looked down at the once proud woman.

"I take it that your current demeanour has not been inflicted by my men" asked the Emperor.

"No of course not" replied Venra. "They have been complete gentlemen." She managed a fake smile. Ignoring her sarcasm he continued.

"The time for games is over Venra. The future of this moon now hangs in the balance. Without the food beacons we will all starve eventually, even the renegade Virtues. Why did he destroy them? Tell me what happened at Devhn-Por." She looked up at the Emperor with contempt.

"As I have told your interrogators for the twentieth time, the Virtue of Air attacked the city and destroyed the ziggurats. He came through the gate. I don't know how. I ran for my life and was shot and left for dead. I managed to crawl aboard a fishing boat and make my way back here, where I thought I would be safe." She glared at Vas.

"I know the story, what I want to know is how you are the only one to survive. Out of the hundreds of soldiers and thousands of civilians you are the only one to make it back alive. Explain that to me."

"What can I say, I am lucky." She tried to flick her long hair but it was stuck to her clothes.

"Do not test me Venra" he snarled.

"Why!" she hollered. "What are you going to do to me? Kill me? Torture me? Go ahead. You have destroyed this moon. There is nothing left here for me or anyone else. Within a revolution we'll all be dead anyway." Her words stabbed at his heart like her poisoned hair pin. He hung his head in overwhelming sadness. After an uncomfortable silence Bela-Sem stepped forward.

"My Lord?" he questioned.

"Take her back to the cells" ordered the Emperor.

*

It took many rotations for Vas to come to terms with his failure. He eventually shrugged off his melancholy shroud and set about planning and providing once more. Over the following revolution the Emperor's forces made only small gains. They had resorted to guerrilla tactics making swift raids across the water, securing food and supplies. Each sortie became more and more dangerous as the Renegade Virtues tightened the noose around the island fortress. His men slowly dwindled in numbers and the words "war of attrition" from the traitorous Principle Sho-Ota continually rebounded inside his head.

All of his actions and decisions had now brought them to this point. The outlaw Virtues now firmly occupied the coast around the island. Their fires now flickered in the distance and they would soon attempt to finish the war by strangling his last stronghold.

Tol-Aka and his remaining Dominators were waiting patiently for him. They were hoping he would come up with a plan that would turn the tide, to spark a glimmer of hope for them to cling to. But he had exhausted his vast reserves of optimism and the reality of what he had done choked him like an aggressive cancer.

The gathered men stood up straight as the Emperor entered the war room.

"My Lord" started Tol-Aka. "We are low on food supplies, but have enough to last us for a short siege. Disease is spreading through the city and we have quarantined those infected in the west quarter. We have enough men to hold the outer walls, although we are running low on arrows and medical rations. Looking at the defences it seems likely that an attack will come from the docks. The rest of the island is sheer cliff, so I would not expect a full scale attack from anywhere else."

"You have done well Tol" complimented Vas. "Despite the cliffs we should still post guards at spaced intervals around the island just in case."

"Of course my Lord" replied Tol-Aka."There is one more thing" hesitated the Virtue. The Emperor saw his reticence.

"Speak plainly Tol, the time for sparing feelings is long gone."

"We were thinking about the great gate" suggested Tol-Aka. The Emperor raised his head sharply. "We could open the gate to the ocean planet, just for food of course. It could provide the resources we need to hold out here." The Emperor looked at the Virtue and then at the gathered Dominators and Principles.

"What do you all think?" he asked. The assembled council looked at each other, looking to each other for a response. It was Bela-Sem that replied.

"The ocean planet is one resource that we have not yet used. It would seem like this could be our final play so anything we can do to lever an advantage would make sense." said the Dominator.

The Emperor drew in a deep breath and lent forward on the mapping table.

"We will defend the outer wall. When that falls we will fall back to the inner bailey. When it looks like we will be overrun there, open the great gate and we will say our final farewells to our home. Bring any of the population who are not showing signs of sickness into the Palace and have them ready to leave. Arm those we must leave behind." Silence held the group. "I am sorry it has come to this my friends. I wanted so much more for this great world. I have brought nothing but death and destruction, but I will not see those who have loyally followed me die here."

The Emperor looked at the faces of his men expecting to see glimpses of disappointment. He saw only affection.

"Life was boring before you became Emperor" replied Tol-Aka with a smile. "You have reminded us of who we are. We are Dumonii and death and destruction pumps through our veins. We will stand against the forsaken Virtues and watch their bodies crash upon our walls. If the time comes, then we will gladly give them this dying world. They will choke in the dust of their ignorance."

*

The Emperor and his Dominators clattered down the stairs to the prison cells following a Reaver who darted through the corridors. They arrived at an empty cell. Two guards lay slumped on the floor, blood clotted around gashes in their necks.

"Venra!" cursed Vas.

"We've sent out a search party, but no reports as yet my Lord" said the Reaver.

"I know where she'll be" replied the Emperor.

Vas and his men ran down through inner bailey and out into the main city. The city covered every patch of ground on the small island. Houses had been built on every available piece of land and when that had run out they built up and down into the rock. It took them some time to wind their way through the maze of houses and down the steep streets towards the docks. The docks had been constructed where the natural bedrock of the island was at its lowest. It also luckily coincided with a natural promontory that formed a natural harbour. Two long arms of wall cupped a deep anchorage. At their furthest point they almost touched leaving only enough space for a single vessel to enter. Behind the dock and several fishermen's houses were the imposing battlements of the outer bailey. The ramparts stretched from the high cliffs on one side across the back of the harbour and up to the cliffs on the other side. To the left of the harbour was a small beach. The stepped pebbles formed a sharp drop into the sea. Countless ropes adorned the beach stretching out into the water. This area was used to winch in nets and pots that were moored off the coast.

Access to this beach was through the huge defences and via a barnacled covered metal gate. As Vas stepped over another dead body towards the open portcullis a dark shape lunged towards him. He batted the spear with open palms so that it skittered harmlessly onto the floor. He then launched his armoured knee into the overstretched face of his adversary. The Dominators drew their weapons and descended the stone steps onto the beach. The tide was low and the stench of seaweed was overpowering. Out to one side on the uncovered rocks were several people. Their silhouettes were illuminated by the flaming torches they waved in the air.

The Emperor and Dominators were quickly picking their way out towards the group. Venra's household put up little resistance to the trained soldiers and they were swiftly dispatched. Vas approached Venra careful not to slip on the blood soaked stones. She backed away the sea lapping at the boulder she balanced upon. She held a short dagger in one hand and a crackling firebrand in the other.

"You're too late!" she scowled.

"I don't think so" replied Vas calmly. "Do you know something? You are probably the best actress I have ever seen, even at death's door you still maintain your masquerade." Venra knew there was nowhere left to hide and the truth spilled out.

"It doesn't matter whether the gate is open or not. The Virtue of Air will still take your sacred island" she hissed.

"That is probably true. I have made my peace with my failures, but what could you possibly hope to gain? You do know Alu-Aka prefers the company of men" said the Emperor raising his eyebrow.

"Of course I know that you fool. It would be the perfect partnership. I would be the queen but without the constant demands of a man in the bedroom. I would be free to live as I pleased. I have lived my life twisting the carnal desires of men to my will. You are weak. You..." Before she could say another word Vas bridged the distance between them and grabbed her hold by the throat with one hand, his other clenching hold of her sword arm. He applied pressure crushing her delicate fingers and the blade rattled off the rocks before splashing into the waves. The Emperor looked into her fiery eyes.

"Weak is one thing I am not" he said evenly. He gradually squeezed the bitterness from her body and then lifting her effortlessly he tossed her backwards into the brine.

Watching on the harbour wall, secreted between two rope pots the small deformed figure of Pol-I wiped the streaming tears from his face.

*

The huge fleet of the Virtues was a jumbled selection of vessels, some hi-jacked seablades but mostly fishing or sailing craft filled to the gunwales with men eager for action. The flotilla made its way across the short gap between the mainland and the port. They were so numerous that they looked to block the island straits forming a continuous floating bridge. They had expected a fierce bombardment as they neared the fortified harbour but they were unprepared for the stone storm that assailed them now.

In behind the main bulwark soldiers heaved back on a rope pulling the weight of the catapult into place. As it neared its marker a large metal pin was hammered into place securing the counterweight. A massive slab of stone robbed from the houses behind was manhandled into place and the sling was fastened around it.

"All clear!" came the shout and the attending soldier brought his hammer down accurately on the holding pin. The colossal weight swung down and the long arm of the trebuchet ratcheted round flinging the stone missile up and over the walls. The Virtue's show of strength now played against him. The tightly packed craft could not manoeuvre, blocked by their comrades on all sides. The reclaimed stone plummeted from the sky crashing right through the wooden mast and splintering the deck of the boat breaking its backbone. The vessel quickly started to sink, the extra weight of the soldiers and their equipment adding to its vulnerability.

The soldiers and civilians of the Emperor worked tirelessly trying to lose as many boulders as they could before the fleet closed range. The barrage was ruthlessly effective in destroying the boats but despite the carnage it claimed relatively few lives. Those not directly hit by the missiles clambered aboard the copious other vessels.

The Emperor and his Dominators were stood on the battlements of the inner bailey watching the satisfying destruction out at sea. From their position they had a panoramic view of the lower city and harbour. From here the Emperor intended to control the battle.

The first few craft now approached the narrow entrance to the harbour. Oarsmen rowed frantically trying to speed past volley after volley of bolt gun fire, arrows, spears and burning pots of tar. The first vessel through was engulfed in fire, flames circled and licked at the mast as the sail cloth blackened and added to the fuel. Soldiers dived into the harbour and swam for their lives. The first wave of vessels all found a similar fate and the mouth to the harbour was filled with floating burning flotsam and desperate cries as the heavy armour of the soldiers dragged them under the water.

To the untrained eye it seemed like madness. A wanton waste of life. To the Virtue of Air it was a simple tactic. The defenders had thrown almost everything they had at these first boats. He had kept the metal hulled seablades back. This second wave of craft now roared towards the gap. The skimming craft tore through the debris and made their way unchallenged into the harbour. Soldiers poured from the vessels and set about securing the way in for their allies.

Inside the main wall a small figure looked cautiously out through an arrow slit. He stood on top of several barrels. He saw the invaders swarm over the piers like a plague of insects devouring all life before them. He heard the wail of compressors high above him as the defenders opened fire in reply. He carefully climbed down from his perch and took a flint from his pocket. He knelt down in front of the explosive kegs like an acolyte at an altar.

"I'm sorry I couldn't save you mistress" wept Pol-l. "I return to you now to be by your side once more." He struck his flint.

From his elevated vantage point the Emperor watched in stunned silence as a massive section of the lower wall exploded out into the harbour. The force of the blast sent rock fragments flying out over the end of the walls. Those guards on top of the defences and those attackers that had been too eager were obliterated in the detonation. Even as remnants of stone were still crashing into the water and smashing into the harbour walls the soldiers of the Virtue were forcing their way through the breach.

"Sound the retreat!" ordered the Emperor. He turned to his Dominators. "We will protect the gate" He said simply.

The two studded gates creaked open and the Emperor walked out onto the cobbled causeway. He drew his two war hammers and clanked them against the two small bucklers secured on each forearm. He stretched his neck, moving his head from side to side. The bell inside the palace tolled and the first defenders could be seen running towards the inner gate. They ran past the iron willed soldiers that stood protecting their withdrawal. Those that made it inside climbed the steps to the battlements ready to fight again when called upon.

Fewer than he had hoped were making it back. The rampaging bloodlust of the attacking force was overwhelming his defenders, cutting them down mercilessly as they ran for their lives. Handfuls of soldiers were still running towards the safety of the palace, but now they were pursed by the enemy.

Bela-Sem skidded past the Emperor his arm held back next to his head as he launched a javelin into the distance. The spear flew over the heads of the retreating soldiers and buried itself deep in the chest of a frenzied soldier splitting his breastbone in two. The small group braced themselves for the first attack.

Metal sang out as weapons clashed on shields and armour. The Emperor unleashed the pent up anger that had been boiling inside him. He fought like a wounded beast with no apparent concern for his own safety. His hammers rose and fell with a hideous rhythm crushing and cracking bone. None could stand before him. His ferocity struck fear into every man that laid eyes on him.

The Dominators inspired by their leader and filled with pride joined the carnage. Bela-Sem whirled his morning star around his head before it collided like a meteor with an unsuspecting skull. The helmet provided no protection as the force of the blow annihilated the man's head. He thrust out his boot at the next soldier catching him in the stomach. The warrior expelled his lungs and staggered backwards. Bela-Sem whipped the metal ball upwards tearing off the helpless victim's lower jaw.

To his right Mot-Sem was hacking his way into the fray brandishing two Khopesh. The forward curving swords fell like meat cleavers ripping through metal and flesh. He ducked beneath an outward strike and chopped at the enemy soldier's knee. The sword tore through bone and ligaments almost severing the limb. He rammed his second sword up under the man's war-kilt. Oblivious to the dying soldier's screams he slashed his sword across the face of the next man. The warrior reacted just in time pulling his head back from the blade. The metal tip cut through his nose bone. He yelled in pain and went to raise he sword to strike. To his horror his arm did not follow his brain's command and he looked down to see a bleeding stump where his right hand had been. It was the last thing he saw as Mot-Sem's Khopesh rent his head from his body.

From behind Mot-Sem a warrior struggled to lift himself from the floor. He was wounded badly but saw an opening on the unprotected back of the Dominator. He drew his knife and jumped. He froze in midair the punching sword of Lo-Sem jutting from his chest. Mot-Sem swivelled and nodded to his brother quickly understanding the situation. Lo-Sem brought his knee up and kicked the dead body from his katar. He ducked as a long bladed pike lashed over his head. He leapt into the air towards the soldier. As he closed the distance he let lose a flurry of punches. The blurred attack punctured the warrior's face and chest with dozens of deep wounds. As the Dominator landed in a crouch he saw the man he had felled was the last of that particular group. At the bottom of the hill the main force was massing. In front of the inner gates more than fifty enemy soldiers lay dead. The Emperor and his men had not lost a single man.

"Inside!" bellowed the Emperor.

Tol-Aka came running from the palace as Vas supervised the closure of the gates.

"The shimmer portal is ready my Lord" panted the Virtue.

"Good" replied Vas. "Get everyone through it."

"There's just one thing" smiled the effervescent Virtue. "Bring a coat, it's freezing down there."

The Virtue and the Principles quickly organised the remaining people and shepherded them through to the portal. The Emperor and his men systematically locked and barred each door into the palace. Unprotected, the high walls of the inner bailey would soon be scaled.

The Emperor slammed the last door. The hum of the gate behind him was overpowering. The portal warped the space at its centre like some invisible phantom wrestling to escape the void.

"That's everyone" reported Tol-Aka. "We have taken as many supplies as we could but it is bitterly cold down there. The island is covered in snow and the sea surrounding it is frozen. We could do with more furs, drapes and fuel for cooking." A loud crack echoed through the chamber.

"We're out of time my friend." replied Vas. "Get through the gate, when the last of us is through, destroy it."

"You are coming, aren't you?" asked the Virtue.

"Of course" placated Vas. "Now Hurry."

The Dominators remained still.

"We're not going anywhere until you go through" stated Bela-Sem.

"This is not a request" said Vas. "I will be along shortly; there is something I must do."

Reluctantly the Dominators filed into the spasming portal. As the last soldier disappeared into the gate the Emperor turned away drawing his war hammers to face the doors which were being hacked apart from the other side.

"Forgive me my friends but I have burdened you for too long."

The door erupted inwards and the Virtue's men poured into the chamber. Vas gritted his teeth and prepared to kill anyone that came close. Before he could die a wasted martyr's death two sets of hands clamped onto his arms and jerked him backwards through the gate.

The shimmer portal hissed and pulsed one last time before it closed forever.

Chapter 9 - Fire and Ice

The group continued to climb up into the clouds. Their progress was slow, hampered by the icy rock. Each step was carefully placed, each new handhold secured before releasing the previous grip. All but Lin had removed their gloves in order to get a better feel for the rock. The rough cliff eventually gave way to smooth mortared block work. The foundations of the great fortress melding with the bed-rock seamlessly. Var could just make out a circular opening just ahead of Hanelore. He hoped they had reached the summit.

Hanelore drew a dagger from his belt and rammed the hilt against the small metal door. The sound rang out and echoed through the interior of the battlements.

"I guess this is where we find out who's home" mumbled Var.

"Whoever it is I'm not climbing down" said Gero.

Hanelore repeated the banging over and over. Var was starting to lose hope when they heard metal scraping behind the doorway. A small slit slid back and two eyes peered through. The small shutter was slammed shut. Bolts scratched against their holders and the door creaked outwards. A blood soaked spear emerged first holding level at Hanelore's throat.

"Don't you recognise me young Konrad" said the old giant.

"Hanelore?" came the question from within.

At last on the brink of freezing to death the tired climbers made their way into the fortress. The young giant slammed the door behind them and re-bolted it. They were in the base of the outer walls and a torch lit staircase led upwards. Hanelore turned to his son.

"Try and stay calm" he insisted.

"When am I not calm?" shrugged Gero.

Konrad led the group up through the fortress. As they made their way through corridors and halls they could see glimpses of destruction through the windows.

"There is a lull in the fighting" said Konrad. "They have not managed to breech the inner wall, although when they have finished constructing their siege towers it may be a different story."

Konrad pushed open two ornately carved wooden doors and inside there were several Magta gathered around a table. Their faces were deep in concentration, which faded quickly with the arrival of the visitors.

"Excuse me Lothair, but I found these vagrants knocking at the back door." announced Konrad. The huge giant looked up and recognition immediately flashed across his weary face.

"I hope you have not come here seeking sanctuary father, as I feel you have hopped out of the fire and into the pot." Hanelore said nothing and walked towards his eldest son and embraced him warmly.

"It's good to see you son" said Hanelore. Lothair stepped back and fixed his gaze on Gero. There was a dangerous silence. He offered his hand.

"Brother" he said plainly. Gero took his hand and shook it. "What are you doing here?" asked Lothair.

"It's a rescue" said Gero gruffly. Lothair stared at his brother and then laughed.

"I'm afraid it's too late for that brother. A few more moons and the army at our gates will overrun our last bastion. We have lost many but we will fight on to the last. I take it you have met the Mer?" asked Lothair.

"We have encountered them briefly" replied Hanelore. "They had bigger things to worry about" he said turning his head and winking at the others. "You may remember this ocean man." Hanelore pointed to Var who stepped forward. "He came before you once several seasons ago to ask for your help. He is the leader of the combined ocean tribes and his quest has led us back here. He has great heart and Gero and I have all pledged our swords to his cause. We must speak with Markus. I hope he is still here."

"He is, but the archive is not. As you will know father the archive lies in the outer bailey. We removed all of the weapons and a great deal of the books. I hope what you search for remains. You are all welcome guests, but I am afraid my hospitality is limited" said Lothair solemnly. "Agmund I did not expect to see you so soon. Have you all returned?" he asked.

"Those of us that live" said Agmund sadly. He retold his story to the shocked Magta leader.

"I have no words" said Lothair. "I cannot imagine what you have been through. I am sorry this is not the safe haven you once knew. Still, you are welcome to stay if you so wish."

"I have seen and experienced more in the last few moons than all my seasons on this planet" said Agmund. "I have pledged my service to Var as I believe he may hold our world in the balance. The days of our people are coming to a close. You could join us?" suggested Agmund.

"That debate has been had my friend. It seems as if we will stay and see out our days here or die trying." replied Lothair.

"You cannot stay here" said Gero with dismay.

"I don't think we would all make it down the route you came in by. Do you brother?" questioned the Titan.

"There is always a way" interrupted Hanelore. "We will talk again when we have found what we are looking for." With that Hanelore ushered the assembled group from the room.

*

They found Markus tending the wounded. He was genuinely pleased to see the old Titan. They exchanged pleasantries and Hanelore explained their purpose at the fortress.

"Gateway to the Gods" chuckled Markus.

"What? Why are you laughing? Does it exist?" questioned Var urgently.

"Oh I am sure it exists" said Markus eying Var intensely. "But finding it would be another matter."

"Tell us what you know about it my friend" asked Hanelore politely.

"The gate was built by the Dumon in their vain attempt to communicate with the Gods of this realm. At the height of their power they felt that they were equals to our deities. That is when the Gods answered those naive taunts and plunged this world beneath the waves. That the gate once existed I have no doubt. Where it is and whether it still exists is far more doubtful."

"It does still exist and its whereabouts are known" replied Var. "It is the key to open it that we search for." Markus cast a serious glance at Hanelore.

"Is this true?" asked the Archive Master. Hanelore nodded.

"So I take it you search for the key in order to confer with the Gods?" he directed the question at Var.

"That's right" said Var vehemently.

"And what would you ask them?" queried Markus.

"I would ask them to save our world" replied Var. Markus smiled.

"I am afraid the books did not say anything about a key. They only refer to the 'chosen' and to the 'guardian'. The chosen is the only one who can open the gate. Once open, the entranceway is protected by a guardian. The chosen must undergo a test of faith and if he is found to be pure of heart then the he will be granted an audience with the Gods. As to who the chosen is or what the guardian is I have no idea."

"Is there nothing else in the books about the key" insisted Var.

"Everything that exists in the pages of those books is duplicated here" said Markus tapping his furrowed forehead. Var sighed.

"We are no closer. We have travelled all this way and still have no idea what the key is or where it might be." complained Var.

"What were you told?" asked Markus.

"I was told I would know the moment I saw it" replied Var.

"We moved all of the precious items from the archive before the outer city fell. I can take you to them, it may be amongst them somewhere."

"Let's go" said Var with renewed enthusiasm.

*

Whilst Var searched the Magta treasure trove for the key, Gero, Agmund, Lin and the brothers found time to rest. Hanelore made his way back to speak to Lothair. They had called those remaining in the council to convene. Hanelore stood to address the gathered members.

"We have lived here away from the world for as long as I can remember. Our reasons for withdrawing were sound, but we no longer live in that same world. We have always despised the Dumon for the blinkered way they stumble through time. We are now no different to them. If our gods truly exist they are in no mood to help us. If we do not act we will die as surely as this planet will follow suit."

Sabine from the Shining Caste stood.

"That is heresy Hanelore."

"Is it?" he retorted. He walked towards the priest. "What does your faith tell you about the dogs at your gate? Will they protect you from them? What about the countless hundreds that have already perished. Who was watching over them when they died?" probed the old giant.

"Those whose faith is resolute still remain" answered Sabine.

"So those who died were lacking in faith?" continued Hanelore. Sabine was unsure of how to answer. "Let me ask you another question then. Is your faith strong Sabine?"

"Of course" replied the priest.

"So strong that it would stop my dagger before it reached your heart?" Hanelore drew his knife and placed the point against Sabine's ribcage.

"Hanelore! That's enough!" shouted Hagon. The older priest rose and placed his hand on Hanelore's blade.

"This is a test of faith your holiness. Surely you would not interrupt" goaded the old Titan. Without waiting for an answer Hanelore plunged the blade into the young priest. The knife punctured his heart and he sagged forward. Hanelore gently lowered him onto the settle.

"What have you done?" roared Hagon.

"I have proved that faith alone cannot save us. We must leave this island and help our ocean friend fulfil his destiny. We must help him find a way to wake the Gods from their eternal slumber. It is a slim hope, but it is still hope. Remaining here abandons all reason and is an insult to all our great forefathers. The Magta were once a great people. It is time we showed why. It is time for us to rejoin the world."

*

Var drew another arrow from the case and notched it to the Nightsigh. The giant's bow was all that kept him from spiralling into melancholy thoughts. He pulled the bowstring back and launched an arrow out over the battlements towards the advancing towers in the distance. He didn't bother to look to see if he had found a target, he knew he had. The arrows never missed.

He had searched all day through the trinkets and ancient artefacts that Markus handed him. None of them looked or felt like a key. He had returned to tell Hanelore the news, but he didn't seem surprised. He was pre-occupied in preparing whatever it was he had dreamt up to combat the advance of the Mer. Gero climbed up behind him and slapped him heartily on the back.

"Alright little Var how many have you bagged?" asked Gero.

"No idea" replied Var. "They seem to be getting closer. Those two towers look finished, I hope whatever Hanelore is cooking up is nearly ready. They will be on us in the morning."

"Should be ready tonight" answered Gero.

As darkness shrouded the fortress the remaining Magta were busy preparing. They had constructed dummies which they were positioning along the battlements. They had equipped these stand ins with weapons and armour. The mock force was now guarding their escape.

To one side of the great keep a mass of wooden scaffolding had been constructed. Its wide base was anchored in the streets and climbed high above the roof tops to form a level platform with the top of the keep. The wooden structure stretched out towards the curtain walls.

Var excitedly followed Gero as they wound their way round the spiral staircase and out onto the roof. Hanelore was busy directing a huge winch. It had already brought up dozens of strange contraptions.

"What are they?" asked Var.

"You'll find out soon enough. We're the first to go. Here tie this around your waist." Gero handed him a leather sling with a metal hook at the front. Var stepped into the harness and then Agmund stepped in and hoisted Var upwards onto Gero's back. He secured the hook and put his arms around the giant's neck.

"Not too tight" coughed Gero. Together they made their way across the roof and the giant hoisted one edge of the large contraption. It was made from thin strips of wood bound together in a triangular shape. The surface had been covered with silk which was stitched securely in place. Gero lifted the wing with ease and underneath Var could see two sets of poles hanging down with wooden bars joining them across the bottom. Gero held onto the bar and secured himself via the same sort of hook and eye to the triangular machine. He turned to look over his shoulder.

"You ready?" he asked smiling.

"For what?" asked Var nervously.

"Ever wondered what it would be like fly?"

Before he had a chance to reply Gero was sprinting out along the wooden ramp. Var could see what was going to happen and closed his eyes tight shut. Gero launched himself off the end of the platform and the spiralling winds instantly caught the hang glider. It sailed silently out over the walls towards the anchored ships in the far distance.

Var felt the freezing air start to crisp his hair and his eyebrows. He opened his eyes. In the darkness he couldn't make out the ground below. He knew it was a long way down. Hanging down from the wing in front of the giant was a small compass. It had a dull glow. Gero kept his eye fixed on the fading light shifting his weight along the bar to keep them on course. Var was grateful it was dark, although it was peaceful. Just the ripple of wind over the material and the creak of bindings. It felt unnatural.

As his eyes adjusted to the low light he could make out the black silhouettes of the waiting ships. Within moments the ice was rushing towards them. Gero had taken his legs out of the rear straps and was hanging on the front bar only. He tried to run as they neared the floor but they were going too fast. He stumbled and the glider smashed into the ice. It dragged them some distance before finally coming to a stop.

"Not my best landing" groaned Gero. Var unhitched himself and helped the giant to his feet. The hang glider was destroyed but it had done its job. Svan approached laughing.

"Hanelore right?" he joked.

"Who else?" replied Gero. They moved the wreckage to one side and prepared to greet the next pilot. Most landed in the same undignified way that Gero had demonstrated, but there were a couple who pulled up at the last moment and managed to run and stop on their feet. They were greeted with a discreet round of applause. A constant stream of Magta and their passengers made their way to the impromptu landing strip throughout the night. Hanelore and Lothair were the last two to arrive.

"Is that everybody?" asked Var.

"All those who wished to come" replied Lothair. "I made out a few figures in the darkness running across the ice. Their gliders must have crashed short. I am amazed so many have made it. The gliders were assembled in haste, I wasn't sure they would make it at all."

"Your father is full of surprises" said Var. Lothair smiled.

Hanelore was staring out over the ice through his spyglass.

"They should be here in time" said Hanelore. "But if we can't free the ships from the ice, it won't make any difference."

They had been away from the yachts for only three moons but the sea ice had already embraced the vessels as its own. The Magta were stabbing at the ice all along the bow of the ship trying to break it up enough so that the sails could pull it free. The ice was almost an arm's length thick and proving to be quite a challenge. They worked through the night chipping away at the icy shackles. No sooner had they freed one section did the plummeting temperatures re-freeze the water. After all the effort they had moved the craft no more than a few ship's lengths. In that time the few stragglers had now caught up.

The first morning rays were clawing at the horizon slowly illuminating a blood red sky. Despite the valiant efforts throughout the night the two ships were stuck fast. Time and energy were running out. Hanelore had suggested that they wait until Shu was high in the sky, the slight increase in temperature would make the task easier, and the winds may increase. As soon as the huge yacht could achieve some momentum its weight would break through its cold trappings and pull itself free. In the bitterly cold wind of the morning that freedom seemed some way off.

The giants had boarded the craft and were huddled together above and below decks conserving energy and warmth. Hanelore his two sons and Var were on a constant look out back across the ice flats. The first call came from high in the rigging. Mort and Mido seemed somehow immune to the temperatures and had been on watch throughout the night. Hanelore adjusted his scope.

"We're out of time" he murmured. Lothair looked through glass and then immediately set about waking the sleeping giants. He organised all those not part of the Destructor caste to renew their attack on the ice stranglehold. The rest armed themselves.

"We have no defences, so we will form a shield point" commanded Lothair. "Hold the line as long as you can. When it folds, retreat to the rear ship and we will defend again from there. We need to give the others as much time as we can to free the ships."

The giants that had a shield formed a wedge, thumping their metal shields into the ice. The remainder took positions in behind. Far out ahead the rumble of charging riders resonated through the sea ice. Var drew his swords and took his place alongside his towering counterparts. Lothair stood to bar his way.

"As I understand it, you and you alone will know the key. Without you we would be simply running blind. You are too valuable and I cannot risk losing you in battle" explained the Titan.

"I think you should understand one thing" started Var. "I answer to no-one, especially you. I have not forgotten your attitude all those seasons ago. Although I respect your kind, in my eyes you have much to repair." With that the small ocean man pushed past the giant leader.

"You'll get used to him" commented Gero following his friend. Lothair walked past the shielded warriors and walked some distance ahead of them. He then crouched on the ice laying his war maul out in front of him.

"What's he doing?" asked Var. "Does he think he can take them all on, on his own?"

"It is for our own safety. The hammer he uses grants him a battle lust that is unmatched on all of Gebshu. But he could unknowingly kill his own as well as the enemy as the thirst for blood blinds him." Var looked again at Gero's brother new respect already blossoming.

Before the Magta could engage the rampaging Shektar, the ice in front of them exploded like a meteor had collided with the surface. Massive chunks of ice rained down as the hideously familiar claws of the Archaos emerged from the crater. The entire ice surface started to undulate as it struggled to hold the monstrous weight. Cracks bolted through the floor like lighting. Huge pieces of ice spewed upwards as the previous smooth surface ruptured. The arrival of the leviathan Archaos had started to achieve what a night of hard labour could not. The Magta working at the front of the ship started to run for the rope mesh hanging down from the ship as the thin ice separated.

"Return to ships" bellowed Lothair as he sprinted full tilt toward them. The Destructor warriors hurried to fill the rear ship as the Archaos struggled to cross the ever moving platform between it and its food. "Get your ship moving father. We will follow on." Var was about to argue his case to remain and help when Gero hoisted him off the floor and leapt from one boat to the other. The sails started to fill and the boat slowly started to slip its moorings.

The second boat struggled. The assembled giants willing the sails to fill and the wind to blow. Before they could follow the ancient beast crashed against the hull. Timber cracked inwards under the impact. The blow had freed the craft but not from the reach of the Archaos. Its imposing pincer smashed through the rigging and clamped around the main mast. With a simple twitch the claws snapped the wood like a tooth pick. The mast fell, toppling over the side and taking several giants with it. It also took away their only means of escape. The secondary pincers of the beast snapped hungrily at the giants as they frantically tried to fend off the creature's multiple limbs.

Ahead of the stricken vessel the crew watched in horror as the Archaos disabled the ship. Hanelore immediately swung the ship hard to starboard.

"We'll not make it back in time!" hollered Var.

"There's another way" said Gero running toward the bow. He lifted a heavy harpoon tip and proceeded to screw it into one of the bars on the modified bolt gun. The harpoon tip had a metal cone head and then four folding flanges that currently lay flat. Var saw his plan and helped tie the heavy anchor rope to the harpoon tip. Gero switched on the compressors. Nothing happened. He stamped angrily on the metal box. It whined briefly. After several more well timed blows the temperamental machines hissed and whirred into life.

"Quickly fire it!" yelled Var.

"I have to wait for the reservoir to fill or it won't make the distance" barked Gero. It seemed like forever waiting for the compressors to build enough pressure.

"That'll have to do" complained the giant. He swung the gun and pointed it back towards the struggling vessel. He aimed upwards and squeezed the trigger. Air gushed out and the harpoon shot up into the air. The rope squirreled out behind it as the weapon arced. It looked briefly like it would fall short, before it eventually smashed through the side of the boat. Hanelore turned the ship once more heading out to the open sea. The arms of the harpoon splayed and the rope twanged tight sending water droplets spiralling along its length. It started to pull the boat free. As it moved the ice beneath the monster broke and the Archaos splashed beneath the surface but not before its flailing claw smashed into the stern of its fleeing prey.

The second vessel was irrevocably damaged and was taking on water at an alarming rate. Hanelore was reluctant to stop just in case the arcane creature had decided to follow. They breathed at last, as they saw the ranks of Merthurian in the distance turn and run towards the shore.

Lothair was the last to leave. He leapt across and within moments the tormented ship sank beneath the waves.

"Let's hope that is the last we see of that thing" said the Titan as he climbed the few steps to the wheelhouse. The celebration was short lived as Var's brother descended quickly from the rigging his young face pale and scared.

"What is it Mort?" asked Var.

"You know what we encountered on the way here? Well I am sure we are some distance from that spot, but there is something very similar in the water ahead. I don't think the currents would have brought it this far south."

"Out of the fire and into the ice is a saying that springs to mind" moaned Gero. They slowed their approach towards the watery graveyard.

"It looks like just Kekken this time. I can see no other bodies, at least at the surface" said Hanelore lowering his scope. Screams came from further up on deck. They ran to investigate and saw a large black animal slink over the side rail. The Magta drew their weapons and were about to cut the lone Kekken down.

"Wait!" yelled Var. He made his way through the barricade of giant bodies towards the animal. It was clearly injured. A long angry wound spread along its thigh oozing green pus. The creature clicked and it attempted to make a sign. It was weaker than he thought and it dropped onto its knees. Var ran towards the dying creature and lifted its talons placing them on his forearms. The mind link struck his mind like thunderbolt and his eyes watered as the pain the animal was feeling flooded into him. He gritted his teeth against the barrage of angst and tried to clear his mind as he had been taught.

<<What has happened?>> Var projected.

<<The division in our colony has become unbalanced. Those of us who wish to stop you reaching the gateway are now

in the ascendancy. A huge shoal waited here for you. They would have taken you to the depths.>>

<<You stopped them?>>

<<We have made a small sacrifice, but in doing so we can no longer provide a safe passage across the open oceans>>

<<What do you mean? We are heading home.>>

<<You cannot use the ocean to travel. My brothers will sense you and hunt you down. You will not be able to overcome their numbers>>

<<What can we do?>>

<<You must make your way to the nearest ice sheet and proceed on foot. You must find the Key and make your way to the Pillars of Itna. It is there that the gateway lies. If we can survive the winter we will meet you there as spring breaks>>

With that the link was broken. The creature clawed its way to the side of the ship and slid over the side and disappeared.

"What did it say?" asked Gero urgently.

"You're not going to like it" replied Var.

*

Toll-Son-Ray watched as his men hurried back towards the main encampment the huge beast stampeding after them occasionally stopping to devour a straggling rider. He nodded to his Captain and Petr and his men spurred their white furred mounts forward. They each carried grappling hooks and swung these round as they made to encounter the Archaos. Surrounding the great creature they threw the hooks over its body, legs and head. Leaping from his mount Petr took a metal spike and mallet from his saddle. He hammered the long pole into the ice and wrapped the snaking rope around it. His men were following suit. The beast was busy mauling on a fallen rider and didn't seem bothered by its fabricated rope cage. Its meal finished it went to raise its claws only to find dozens of strands tethering them to the ground.

In a swift movement it exerted its strength and ripped the ground anchors free sending men and Shektar flying in all directions.

"Get more ropes on it" yelled Petr. The free claw snapped randomly at the men trying to right themselves. It caught one soldier mid air clipping him in two. The creature moved again ripping more lines from the ice, but as soon as one came free another hook looped over it and was added to the restraints. The soldiers milled around the trapped animal darting in at any perceived safe point to hack at its body.

The Red Prime Captain took hold of a loose rope and ran towards the creature. The huge pincer followed him threatening to slice him open. He jumped avoiding the snip and landed on one of its rear legs, he used the rope and quickly climbed onto its carapace. He removed a small axe slung around his back and arced his back using all his force to bring it to bare. The blade chipped some of the crustaceans from its shell but otherwise made no impression. He searched for a weak spot. He could see wrinkled skin underneath the head plate where it joined the body. There was no way near it as its bony spines tore through the air as it thrashed its head making any attempt certain suicide. He signalled to one of his men down on the ice.

"Throw me some spikes and a hammer" he yelled over the noise of the creature's howls. He deftly caught the tools and set to work hammering the metal staves into the creature's shell. It took several attempts but the thin points eventually punched their way through. By now several other soldiers had joined their captain and were mirroring his actions. The creature didn't seem to feel anything as they sunk spike after spike through its carapace.

Once he had several staves buried home he cut one of the hook ropes and wound it around the ends of the metal pegs. He secured the other end of the rope around his arm.

"Spear!" he yelled once more. Obeying instantly a long spear was cast up to him. He braced himself with the rope and threw the spear at the soft tissue. The Archaos felt this new attack and roared in anger. It swung its head skidding soldiers across the ice and then lifted it upwards using its two pincers as leverage. It tore free from its bonds and furiously started to club the Mer into the ice with its claws. It shook its body trying to dislodge the parasites that clung for their lives to its back.

Petr was thrown to one side and landed heavily against the creature's side. His grip remained firm on the rope and grabbing a broken spear sticking out from between the body segments he ripped it free and climbed once again onto the creature's shell. His men had already cast several more javelins and spears into the soft skin. Black pungent blood crept from the wounds. He took the spear and releasing his rope he ducked beneath a bony spine as the creature still thrashed. He wedged the half spear under the head plate and kicked the wooden shaft until it was upright. Again his men followed his lead. Before the creature had a chance to crush the bracing he slid under the plate and grabbed at one of the protruding weapons. He stabbed it back into the wound this time pushing it as deep as he could. The creature threw back its head snapping the makeshift supports. It bellowed as it felt pain for the first time in its long life. As its head pitched from side to side trying to dislodge the cause of its irritation it threw Petr clear. He rolled to break his fall and ran clear as the creature's legs continued to pound into the ice and snow.

"This thing just won't die" he yelled. The creature confused by the pain it felt was turning and attempting to return to the safety of the water. The stubborn Mer had no intention of letting it go. 'I need a bigger weapon' thought Petr as he glimpsed one of his men take an enormous swing with a two handed axe. He ran through the stamping legs and grabbed the axe from the confused soldier. Ducking and weaving he slung the axe over his back and jumped for a loose rope. Climbing once more onto the creature's back he tried a new approach. He tied the rope to his belt and lent out over the animal's rear legs. With the two handed axe high over his head he brought it down on the leg joint. The weight and keen edge of the weapon sank into the protective cartilage.

Like a man possessed he thumped the axe repeatedly into the same area opening up a serious wound. As his last strike fell the few sinews holding the leg in place snapped and the weight of its own leg saw it fall free. A cheer went up from the Mer as they watched the giant segmented leg crash into the snow.

Soldier after soldier now climbed the dangling tethers eager to join in the victory. They hacked, slashed and stabbed at the leg joints and the giant creature eventually fell onto the ice. Petr gathered a spike and grabbed a spear. He leapt through the spines and climbed onto the creature's head, his bloody visage reflected in the creature's eyes.

Taking another spike he hammered it into the skull. Only his primeval determination saw him succeed in sinking the spike through the thick shell. The creature's throes started to weaken as the army of soldiers crawled over the disabled creature hacking at every opening. Petr drew the spike clear and rammed the spear into the hole. He jumped high into the air grabbing the top of the shaft and using his weight skewered the weapon into the animal's brain. It twitched briefly as it struggled to understand what had happened before collapsing, its ancient life extinguished.

Toll-son-ray rode out towards the carnage. He reigned in his mount and slowly padded towards the panting captain.

"Well done captain. You certainly live up to the stories told about you. A more gifted warrior I have yet to see." Petr bowed, too tired to answer. "When you have recovered, rejoin your men in the North. As soon as the ice is thick enough you know what to do." He turned to another painted warrior. "What news?"

"They escaped, but the creature took one boat" answered the soldier.

"That's a shame." He turned to his captain once more."We must pray for storms Petr, or you may have more of a challenge than we bargained for. I will follow the freezing ice with the main force as soon as we have plundered the citadel. We will cleanse this world. Nothing can stand against us." He spat onto the dead carcass, pulled his scarf up over his nose and then wheeled his Shektar away.

Chapter 10 - Home

Not wanting to return into the clutches of the Archaos or the Mer, Hanelore headed for the nearest land, Dilmuna. The sea ice had spread some distance around the island and the crew were reluctantly disembarking from the comfort of the ship.

"We could just take our chances on the ocean" suggested Lothair.

"I have seen firsthand what these creatures can do. I would not wish that on my enemy. If we have to walk to avoid them, then I'll make my peace with that" said Agmund.

"The Kekken have proved their worth before. I have no way of knowing what they say is true or not. But our minds were linked and I felt no sense of betrayal or deceit" added Var.

"Then walk it is" said Lothair.

"Who said anything about walking?" grumbled Hanelore. "We can use the boat to build at least six ice yachts. We can travel as fast across the ice as we can on the water. It may take a while to build them that's all." The suggestion was met with widespread enthusiasm and the Magta rapidly organised themselves into groups. Some to dismantle the ship and build, some to fish for food and the rest set out towards the island to find shelter. Var and Gero joined the latter group. Var was sure he had seen the island before but under a blanket of snow it looked different.

They trudged through the deep snow, heads bent down avoiding the freezing wind blowing over the island. It was impossible to tell when they had cleared the ice and met land as the snow was so thick. The going was difficult. Var kept to the back. Walking in the footprints of the giants made it slightly easier. The stump of his leg was sore and he ached to remove the prosthetic limb and slink into a water bath. That image kept him going until they crested the first rise on the small island. Gero was leading and immediately thrust himself prone into the snow. Var crawled past the other giants and made his way up next to his friend. Ahead up in rocky hills were hundreds of people.

They were ill equipped for the elements and wore an assortment of what looked like fine drapes and curtains pulled tightly around their shoulders. They had made use of the few caves that littered the scree. Most were huddled at the mouth of the caves around small fires. Gero could see that there was a large swathe of fir trees missing lower down on the island.

"If they intend burning their only building material, they won't last long" whispered the giant as he turned to Var. Var was gone. He had made his way out around the rocks and was walking towards the strange group. "Stay here. If this goes wrong fetch the others" Gero rasped.

Var could not understand why the people he approached looked at him in fear. Then he turned behind to see Gero striding towards him. He shook his head.

"You'll scare them" complained Var.

"Who me?" said the giant innocently. He looked up at a group of people running towards them down the hill, their black armour clearly showing under their makeshift wraps.

"I don't think they're that scared" said Gero shrugging his shoulders.

Var's heart sank as he recognised the man leading the pack. He was tempted to draw his swords but decided against it. The oncoming group however did not hesitate and they drew an assortment of weapons as they slowed their approach. The tall leader signalled to his group to halt. He walked forwards on his own to confront Var.

"You!" he snarled. "I had hoped never to see your face again."

"I can't say I am happy to see you either" replied Var struggling to remain calm.

"Gentlemen" intervened Gero. "Let's keep this cordial. We can ill afford further enemies and it seems as if you and your people have enough on your hands." Gero looked at the thin faces around him.

"What do you mean?" demanded the man "We are ready to die if that is what is called for."

"I am merely observing that your people are not best equipped for these conditions. Bloodshed would only make this situation worse" stated Gero. The man relaxed and lowered his war hammers. He moved a catch and they simultaneously folded away.

"Stand down" he commanded.

"We are just passing by" started Var. "We will keep our distance and will not bother you. When we saw you I thought you could use our help. It seems as if some of your people are starving." The tall man looked anguished. Var turned to leave.

"Wait.... Please" said the Emperor. "You say you are passing by. Where is it that you are heading?" Var remained cautious.

"We are heading North. We must remain a few moons as we have various tasks to complete" he said warily.

"You know who I am don't you?" asked lord Vas.

"Yes" said Var."You are the brother of the man I killed and the son who killed his own father."

"That is true" replied Vas. "I am also the Emperor, though that means very little in this God forsaken place" He reached into his coat. Gero flinched, his hand reaching for his axe. The Dominators reacted looking to draw their own weapons. The Emperor slowed his movements and gradually withdrew a silver necklace from inside his garments. "This is the seal of the Emperor. It has been passed down from father to son since our civilisation was founded. It now finds itself in my hands. The last Emperor. We ran from a glorious death only to find a slow demise here on this frozen planet. Whatever I am I have much to answer for. Judgement will be passed on me before my life is ended, of that I am sure."

Vas's admission swept over Var as he was transfixed on the seal in the Emperor's hand.

"The Key" he muttered.

"What?" said Gero.

"It is the key we have been searching for. They said I would know it when I saw it. That is it." said Var. Reaching automatically towards the trinket. The Emperor tucked it back inside his coat.

"Key?" he asked. Var hurriedly explained about the Kekken, the gateway to the Gods and the key. Lord Vas listened closely. He eyed the ocean man for some time.

"Our civilisation has always found its base in the strength of men. If you can prove yourself and defeat me in combat the seal is yours." He said finally.

"I would happily pound your arrogant face into the snow" said Gero clenching his fists.

"It's alright my friend" calmed Var. "This is my fight. Besides I think it is personal for the Emperor." He removed his outer fur coat and handed it together with his twin swords to Gero. The Emperor in turn handed his weapons to a Dominator. The two men circled each other carefully finding their feet in the snow feeling for anything that might throw them, each trying to measure the other. The two fighters could not have been more mismatched. Vas was tall with huge upper body strength a master of combat brought up from birth in martial violence and battle. Var in contradiction was wiry with long straggly hair showing his roots as an ocean tribesman, raised by a caring and loving family and until only a few seasons previous had not encountered death or violence. In that time however he had seen and experienced more than most and this had furnished him with a steel determination.

Vas launched himself forward feigning a low kick but then jumping and spinning around firing out a backfist as he did. The ferocity and speed of the attack caught Var off guard and he spun from his feet as the Emperor's fist connected with his jaw. He rolled into the snow and wiped the blood from his lip as he stood. The Emperor attacked once more in a blur of kicks to the body the final roundhouse slapping Var across the face. This time he remained on his feet but a fresh trickle of blood ran from his nose.

Var tried to remember what Gero had taught him. 'Always keep a level head, never lose your temper' had been his advice, but he was struggling to keep his rising anger in check. He blocked another fierce set of kicks by hammering down with his elbows and bringing his knees up. The power of the kicks rocked him from side to side.

Var saw an opening and shot out with a jab. Vas blocked it with an open palm and then stepped back to avoid the follow up upper cut. As the punch sailed harmlessly through the air, the Emperor attacked Var's open midriff. The blow hit the ocean man like a boulder and as the air escaped from his lungs he doubled over. He couldn't stop the Emperor's knee as it thundered into his face. The blow knocked him backwards and stars danced across his vision.

"Stay down" ordered Vas.

Var tried to shake his eyesight clear, sending a crimson spray across the snow from his shattered nose. He bared his teeth showing a bloody grin. He jumped forward turning his hips over swinging his leg with all his weight. His artificial leg cracked against the Emperor's thigh like a war club. The blow shocked Vas, and he hopped back, his leg numb and stinging with pain.

"That was a surprise wasn't it" goaded Var. He tried the same thing again hoping to compound the Emperors injury. A lower blow could smash his knee. Var's anger was slowly taking over and he telegraphed the shot. Vas jumped backwards slapping the kick downwards he then struck with a hard left into Var's kidneys and followed up with an upper cut that lifted the lighter man from his feet. He fell hopelessly into the snow struggling for consciousness.

"You have proved your point, now stay down" said the Emperor. Gero made to help the fallen warrior. Var pushed him away fighting through the pain, raw hatred now powering his bruised and battered body. He ran directly at the Emperor grabbing him around the waist and sending them both tumbling backwards into the powder. He tried to press his charge and rained down punch after punch towards his foe's head. The Emperor used his legs to grab the wild man around the chest and guard himself against the attack. A couple of shots made it through before he grabbed Var's arm and rolled. He quickly reversed the situation and knelt into his back grabbing the coughing ocean man around the throat. He flexed his huge arms and the sleeper hold finally stopped the struggling Var.

The Emperor stood and returned to his Dominator as Gero rushed to Var's side. Gero reached down and cradled his friend lifting him up with ease.

"Does that make you feel better?" rasped Gero as the Emperor returned putting his jacket back on. He took out his seal and draped it over the unconscious Var. Gero didn't understand.

"But he lost?" said Gero

"Strength is not just a test of the physical body" replied Vas. "He has a heart that beats with the fury of a thousand stars. I needed to be sure of who I was dealing with. When he wakes tell him my people and I would like to join his cause. If he would allow it." With that Vas and his entourage left to return to their business.

*

"What is it?" asked Var.

"Looks like one of those beasts we fought back at the fortress. Doesn't look to be moving though" replied Gero. The two men were venturing out across the sea ice on a fishing trip when they had spotted the anomaly on the level surface.

They approached the fur mound with caution and as they neared they saw a smaller Shektar nuzzling against its fallen parent. It turned and curling back its lips revealed its teeth, growling as they drew closer.

"I think this chap may be an orphan" suggested the giant. It backed against its mother as the two men circled the beast. Even as a young pup it was up to Var's waist.

"What do you reckon?" asked Var.

"It would make a welcome change from fish for our supper. It would probably feed the whole c amp" replied Gero.

"No, not about the dead one. The youngster. Those soldiers rode them, so they must be open to training. It would certainly make a good look out."

"Well, that's your responsibility. If it bites me, I can't promise it won't end up in the pot" grumbled the giant. Var took a piece of dried salted fish from his pack and held it out towards the animal. It looked at him with interest. He threw the morsel in front of it. The creature moved forward and sniffed the treat. Its long black tongue shot out and devoured the meal.

"He likes fish" grinned Var excitedly. He could see the giant was already getting impatient waiting to skin and butcher the dead mother. Var held out another piece of food towards the pup and this time it took it carefully from his hand. As he did so, Var gently stroked the animal on the back of its head making sure his hand was well away from the dangerous jaws. He fed the young Shektar a few more pieces before slipping a leather strap over its neck. He tempted the animal from his parent with more dried fish before throwing a piece ahead. The animal nearly jerked the lead from his hand and Var sprinted after him. He led his new found friend back towards the camp.

"Send someone out to help me bring this carcass back" Gero yelled after him, but Var was already too distracted.

Gero returned later that afternoon just as the pale light was fading. He saw the young pup tethered outside Var's igloo chomping on a large fish head. Var bounced towards him.

"Here let me help you with that" he said cheerfully. The fact that the giant had been out on the ice all the while, skinned and dissected the animal, then dragged it all the way back all on his own seemed to escape his friend. Gero just shook his head as he handed two large chunks of meat over to Var.

*

As the small group of giants huddled around the glowing coals later that evening, Hanelore used a sword to flip the sizzling slab of meat.

"Smells good" said the old giant. He turned to Var who was tugging at the stitches in his mouth. "So Var, what are you going to call your new pet?"

"I have named him Hotay." replied Var. "It's a name I remembered from the stories I was told as a child about the old gods." He continued to pick at his healing wound.

"Well!" exclaimed Gero. "Tell us the story then." Var laughed.

"Are you warm enough?" he joked. Gero just glared at his friend. "Well then I'll begin. The king of all the gods, the great Shu had two sons Hotay and Lugh. The day came when one of his sons would have to take his place and rule over the world. Shu designed a race to help him decide which son he should choose. He told them they must compete in this race and the winner would be the new ruler. He also told them that win or lose they would each suffer a terrible famine. They agreed to the terms and set off on the race. There wasn't much difference in the brother's physical ability and they remained neck and neck throughout the race. As they neared the finish line they each saw a wooden cage on the side of the track. Each cage contained a male and female goat. Both brothers remembered what their father had told them and stopped.

Lugh opened the cage and swiftly broke the necks of the beasts. He slung them over his shoulder and continued. Hotay took his time to tether the animals and chased after his brother leading the two live animals. Lugh won the race and shouted up to his father. I have won. I should now rule this world. His father answered saying that he had indeed finished first, but as agreed would now suffer a terrible famine as would his brother. After only a small way through the famine Lugh had eaten the goats that he had killed and he starved to death. Hotay who had kept the animals alive lived off their milk and then their offspring and managed to survive the famine. His father rewarded him by crowning him king of the world. He said that only a person who could plan for the future was worthy to rule."

"That's a good tale" said Gero. "But by the way that new animal of yours eats; it will be you who has to survive a terrible famine".

*

It was deep into winter before the ice yachts and the many sleds that would be needed to transport the Magta and Dumonii towards Imercia were ready. The sea ice had eventually spread out across the ocean and Hanelore was confident they would be able to travel North and return to the city of Asturia without crossing open water. Open ocean was no longer an option for them anyway as Hanelore's ship had been completely recycled to form their new method of transport.

The amount of people that would be undertaking the arduous journey had now tripled as Var had accepted the Emperor's offer. Even though this added a statistical burden the Dumonii learnt quickly and soon were a productive force matching the output from the giants. They organised themselves efficiently and joined the Magta teams fishing and building. They learnt the skills they would need to stay alive in the harsh white environment.

Var realised that his old adversary had probably needed his help more than he would ever had admitted. He looked back at his humiliating defeat at the hands of the Emperor. Perhaps this was the only way he could position himself to ask for help and still save any semblance of respect from his people. They had a totally different mindset and simply did not tolerate weakness or indecision.

Var spent time getting to know the Emperor, understanding the sequence of events that had brought the two men together for a second time in their lives. He built new respect for the man he would have once killed without a thought. He listened to his broken plans and the shattered dreams for his people and realised they weren't too distant from his own. Var's new found trust of the Emperor and the Dumonii was not shared by the Magta. Although they worked in harmony as soon as tools were downed they returned to eat and socialise separately. Despite Var's best efforts the race of giants felt uneasy over the alliance.

Conditions were becoming increasingly harsh as temperatures plummeted and heavy snow fall became constant. Despite the weather, excitement started to buzz through the encampment as the time for leaving the small island that had been their home for the last thirty moons approached. With a good wind they would make it back to Asturia, re-supply and then travel

North. Conditions allowing they could then head South to reach the Pillars of Itna before spring arrived to thaw the ice.

*

The magnificent yachts creaked and cackled as they were loaded. Hanelore explained that the new constructions would need time to bed into their bindings and joints. They had almost deforested the island of Dilmuna in providing timber for the extra craft. The giants were at odds with what seemed like reckless plunder, but were convinced that their actions were appropriate to the desperation of the situation. There would be no point in leaving a steady crop for fuel and construction if there was no-one left to make use of it. Regardless of race the six hundred plus souls were now keen to make their exodus.

Besides the nine huge passenger ice yachts they had also built two smaller versions. These had been used to transport groups far out onto the ice to fish, but now they would be used as originally intended to scout ahead of the migration. Var had learnt to pilot these small vessels and his skill had started to match the experienced sailors of the Magta. Now, much to the annoyance of Hanelore he was racing out across the ice away from the preparation. The morning had seen a particularly heavy snowstorm and in the chaos of dismantling the camp Hotay had broken free from his leash. Var knew exactly where he was going. He had been a constant companion on all of their fishing trips South of the island. Gero and Var had to wrestle the fish away as soon as they dragged them up through the holes in the ice, else the young Shektar would have snaffled them up. He had then taken to diving beneath the ice and catching his own. As they had continued their trips Hotay had become by far the more successful fisherman.

Var controlled the craft as it skidded and bumped over the ice and snow. Despite the fresh snowfall he could still see the deep grooves made by the skids on previous trips and in the centre were loping paw marks. Ahead he could see Hotay furiously raking at the ice trying to open a previous hole. Var had bonded well with the creature and it had responded well to training. However it still had a mind of its own and at the moment food was its number one priority. Var slowed the vessel and the furry animal raised its head sniffing the air. Var approached without concern.

"Hey boy!" he shouted. The young Shektar ignored him still sniffing the air. Hotay started to growl. "It's okay boy, what's the matter? What can you smell?" Var didn't need an answer. As he looked into the near distance he saw the disturbed snow wisping into the air.

"Quick Hotay! Get on the yacht." Var grabbed the beast's collar and led him back to the craft. He placed a smoked fish on the deck and Hotay happily settled down to munch on the free meal. Var swung the boom and urged the sail to fill. The ice had started to vibrate as the oncoming horde thundered towards him. The lithe vessel picked up speed and Var tacked as efficiently as he could trying to stay ahead of his pursuers. The island loomed into view and he could see the tall masts lining up in the frozen bay. He careered into the busy scene, sending people diving in all directions. He hauled on the brake and crashed into the side of one of the passenger yachts showering those already boarded in ice shards.

He scrambled from the craft.

"Mer!" he yelled as Gero and his father ran to see what the fuss was about.

"How many?" asked the old giant.

"I don't know, all of them I guess" replied Var. "They'll be here any moment." His tone of urgency attracted the other leaders and Lothair and Vas came running over.

"We will have to make our stand here then" said Lothair calmly. "We don't have time to finish loading. Besides I have had enough of running. This time it's all or nothing."

"They will be expecting a few hundred of your people Lothair" said Vas. "They will not be ready for hundreds more seasoned warriors."

"Good point" conceded the Titan. "We will form a shield wall and take the brunt of the charge. We can then open gaps allowing your men to attack. They must keep their forays brief and then return to the safety of the shield wall. We can repeat this and hopefully we can whittle down their numbers without losing too many of our own."

"Agreed" stated Vas. The alliance moved frantically, grabbing weapons and shields that had already been stowed. Most ran out onto the battlefield un-armoured. The giants formed a moving triangle with the Dumonii in behind. They had to run at full tilt to keep pace with the huge Magta warriors. Var was struggling to keep up. He had given up trying to tell Hotay to stay and the animal was bounding obediently behind its master.

As the Mer army came into sight the Magta crashed their shields into the ice and braced their shoulders against them. Vas and his men drew their weapons and crouched out of sight behind their allies. Gero looked out over the top of his shield. He looked to his brother.

"Looks like you thinned their numbers further than you thought" said Gero.

"Let's hope that's all there is" replied Lothair.

Unbeknown to the defending soldiers Toll-Son-Ray had indeed only sent part of his force to pursue the fleeing giants. His main force had split in two, part heading North to rejoin Petr and the Red Prime and the rest he had assigned to hunt down and destroy the Magta. Notwithstanding his mistake the charging Mer outnumbered their quarry two to one.

As they neared the ice started to shake. The giants linked arms and hankered down to avoid the scattered showers of arrows coming from the approaching riders. Only a third of the Merthurian force was mounted the rest had been towed behind them on long sleds. These had been abandoned and the infantry ran in the white flurry kicked up by the Shektar.

"Hold the shield wall!" shouted Lothair. "Only release on my order."

The ground shook violently. The war cries mixed with the roars of the Shektar and made hearts pound as they prepared for the inevitable collision. The mounted force battered into the giant's shields knocking them backwards. Thudding and thumping all along the line. Although pushed back the giants held firm helped by the Dumonii lending their weight to the resistance.

With the charge slowed the mounted riders lashed out with swords and spears and their mounts reared up trying to crash through the blockade.

"Open!" hollered the Titan. Those that couldn't hear over the din of battle followed suit as the openings rippled along the triangle of shields. From out of the gaps rushed the Dumonii. Stabbing and slashing into the massive furred targets. Dragging riders from their saddles and trampling them underfoot as they quickly withdrew. The shields closed in a unified metal clunk and once again the Shektar and their riders fell upon the barricade trying to claw their way through. The Magta held this time pushing back against the animals.

The cry came again from Lothair and the killing gaps opened to release the freshly prepared warriors behind. There was the temptation to stay outside the shield wall as the blood lust grew, but Vas's men were well drilled and withdrew each time of asking. The tactic continued and proved incredibly successful. The charge had faltered. Hundreds of animals and men were already bleeding onto the ice, whilst other animals ran or circled rider-less unsure of what to do. Those still able, drew back from the immoveable obstacle and joined the foot soldiers who were now ready to join the fray. Lothair watched carefully as the enemy forces massed. He turned to Vas who was crouching close behind him.

"You're sure you can do this?" he asked.

"Watch and learn, my friend" replied Vas.

"I will be right behind you if you don't make it" growled Lothair.

"That makes me feel so much better. Now let's do it" bellowed Vas.

Lothair stood thrusting his hammer into the air.

"Vanguard!" he yelled.

Hearing the command, the giants at the far ends of the triangle started to move forward. As they charged forward the centre remained still having the effect of straightening the line. As the Mer saw the movement it spurred them into action and they rushed to meet their enemy in combat. As the swords and axes rang out the Magta at the centre of the battle moved aside. Through the gap poured Vas and his Dominators. With the majority of the huge Shektar dead or maimed, the group of expert warriors pummelled into their adversaries.

Vas led his men with skill and fury. Hammer blow after blow cracking unprotected skulls. Those that wore metal helms fared no better as he deftly spun the weapon in his hand striking with the reverse point instead of the hammerhead. The metal spike struck through one man's helm sinking deep into his brain. As he fell, the weight of his body took Vas's hammer with it. He used his forearm buckler to fend off blows as he struggled to free his weapon. Ker-Sem seeing his leader's weapon stuck fast lashed downwards with his two handed sword. The massive blade easily severed the dead warrior's head. Vas felt the weight diminish and brought his second hammer to bare. He thumped a blow into the Mer soldier in front of him smashing the decapitated skull that had been stuck on his hammer spike. The repulsion that the defending man felt was short lived as Vas rammed the edge of his buckler into his bloody face.

Their plan was simple. Vas and his Dominators would carve a line straight through the ranks of the Merthurian. When they made it through the arms of the Magta line would bend, closing in around the trapped fighters. With nowhere to run they would be slaughtered.

Vas had no intention of ever losing another battle. He would die here on the ice or smash his way through as promised. Along the line of Magta the rest of the Dumonii soldiers now fought side by side with their giant counterparts.

Lothair had followed Vas and his men into the death pit, his aim to keep them from being overrun from behind as they drilled into the battle. His war maul glowed brightly as he swung the weapon with both hands in a wide circle. His muscles pumped with the power that the weapon bestowed upon him. Bodies flew like rag dolls as the rounded hammer head powered through the ranks of Mer. Lothair let the euphoria take him completely and he became as one with the devastating weapon. He spun and moved as if dancing on the ice every movement with purpose every strike crumbling the bones of his victims.

Var had held the rear of the triangle at the start. He, his brothers, Gero and Lin had fought sporadic battles with those who had sought to circle around and attack from behind. As they had moved forward Var has lost contact with his friends. He stood between two giants using their shields as cover before jumping and hacking with his two short swords. They had been given to him seasons ago by Hanelore. They were ancient weapons of the Magta and the crude forward sloping blades could cut through anything.

He leapt from behind a shield and chopped down at a Mer soldier who was trying to block a strike from the giant. The blade sliced clean through the knee and the man toppled forward. Var brought his second blade upwards chopping the front of the helpless man's face off. His white teeth and eyes stood in stark contrast to his bloody visage. Var jumped back, balking at the site. As he turned his head away he saw a mounted warrior charging towards their flanks. He broke formation and ran to meet the lone rider. Seeing the blood drenched Var heading to meet him, the Mer soldier hauled on the reigns of his steed aiming the howling Shektar towards Var. He drew back his arm and hurled a spear. The ocean man dived to one side as the spear chunked into the ice. His momentum paused, the Shektar bore down on him. He sprinted and then jumped onto his knees skidding towards the charging beast. He ducked the snapping jaws of the animal as he slid under its body, at the same time slashing out with both swords. The weapons carved through flesh and bone severing the animal's front legs. As the Shektar crashed into the ice he lurched to the right. He almost made it out from under the tumbling beast but his leg was trapped, his good leg.

The rider of the fitting animal climbed over its body and seeing Var trapped, jumped onto his chest. Var had dropped one of his mattocks in the encounter so swung the other. The Mer warrior lent back as the wild swing missed. He lunged with his own axe as Var reversed his attack. At the last moment his short sword blocked the axe blow. The collision sending both weapons bouncing out across the ice, his attacker pounded down with a flurry of punches. Var desperately struggled to defend himself as the man attempted to draw a boot knife. In a white blur the weight of his enemy was lifted from his chest. He kicked against the now dead beast and finally released his foot. He rolled to the side to see Hotay with his jaws firmed clamped around the Mer's neck.

Vas ducked low and then shoulder charged the soldier in front of him. He skidded back onto the ice. He could see that there was no-one behind him. His Dominators filed through and they turned now ready to close the circle. Those Merthurian that saw what was happening made to bolt for freedom. A couple made it through before the death noose started to tighten. With no place for the Mer to retreat the Magta and Dumonii pushed inwards.

Lothair was at the eye of the storm, his whole body encased in a eerie glow, his war maul siphoning the life-force from his victims as he smashed their bodies and their will. The final moments of the battle moved quickly as the remaining Mer were cut down as some tried to surrender or beg for mercy. After the horrors of the Fortress of Ages no quarter was given.

Gero wiped sweat and blood from his forehead and he looked to see only friends standing. He moved towards his brother but before he could call out Lothair spun and the power hammer slammed into his chest. The blow felled the giant as easily as it had toppled the Merthurians. The instant Lothair saw his brother's face he knew he could not stop the swing. As Gero fell backwards Lothair dropped the cursed weapon the battle spasm immediately subsiding. Tears now replaced the bloodlust to cloud his vision.

"Nooo!" shouted the Titan.

Epilogue

Bronsur looked into the mirror on her bedside table. Her mother of pearl teeth shone much brighter than her natural ones. She closed her mouth and brushed her hair. Buttoning her blouse she made her way down the hallway. As she approached the steps an out of breath Yenga came running up. Since Var had been away Yenga and Bronsur had become good friends. Yenga had arrived with Jed and Lin and was keen to prove her worth. Despite her youth she was intelligent and measured and Bronsur had found a useful friend and advisor in the young woman.

"They are..." panted Yenga. "They are all waiting."

"Take a breath girl" slowed Bronsur. "It is customary for the host to keep their guest waiting for a moment. Especially if he is as good looking as you say."

"Oh he is" replied Yenga. The young woman filed in behind Bronsur as the two made their way to the main hall of the keep. The tribal Helmsmen and most of the senior ocean tribes people were present as had become the custom when greeting new visitors to Asturia. Bronsur, with all the dignity and poise of someone who had been in charge for centuries, sashayed her way across the hall.

"Welcome to Asturia. I am Bronsur-Aon-Vieto. My husband is the Doyen of this city. I am afraid he is away currently so it is I you may deal with."

The man held her gaze. He had bright emerald eyes and long hair tied tightly behind his head. His jaw was chiselled and his high cheekbones gave him a princely air. Despite the wind chapped skin around his eyes he was every bit as good looking as Yenga had said.

"It is my pleasure" replied the man. "I am known only as Petr. My tribe and I have travelled a long way to be here. Life in the South has become hard to say the least. I was hoping that you could extend your hospitality to us for a while, at least until the winter has passed.

"That will be our pleasure" replied Bronsur.

www.ingramcontent.com/pod-product-compliance
Lightning Source LLC
Chambersburg PA
CBHW020104030726
47498CB00006B/1937